PRAISE FOR *TALKING ANIMALS*

"Joni Murphy's inventive and beautiful allegory
depicts a city enmeshed in climate collapse, blinded
to the signs of its imminent destruction by petty hatreds
and monstrous greed: that is, the world we are living
in now. *Talking Animals* is an Orwellian tale of
totalitarianism in action, but the animals on this farm
are much cuter, and they make better puns."
—Chris Kraus, author of *I Love Dick* and *After Kathy Acker*

"The best NYC novel since *The Puttermesser Papers*,
Murphy's wise and hilarious *Talking Animals* bobs along
the wake of the present and coming floods like some
driftwood ark of sibylline genius. Its beasts reveal ourselves:
the mercenaries, the easily complicit, the legion of sheep
and lemmings (no offense), and the rarely defiant.
Read it; after all, the sky is falling."
—Eugene Lim, author of *Dear Cyborgs*

"Set in a world as cruel and complex as our own, Joni
Murphy's *Talking Animals* erases the illusory distinction
between man and beast. This tale of lonesome hearts, rising
seas, and political intrigue is not only engrossing and finely
wrought, it carries a message of survival: we're all in this
together, and we need each other."
—Lisa Locascio, author of *Open Me*

"Absurd and irreverent, *Talking Animals* is a wild love letter to all bureaucrats, academics, and alpacas of the anthropocene. Joni Murphy, rightful zookeeper-heir to Kafka's animal kingdom, speaks for us all."
—Patty Yumi Cottrell, author of *Sorry to Disrupt the Peace*

"The long effort to raise human life above all else comes to a merciful end in Joni Murphy's *Talking Animals*. Grief, inequality, the possibility of liberation: Murphy sings a song 'not kind, just true.' This is a rare novel, one with the humane gift of humor—and real urgency. And rarest of all, it's a novel we need."
—Andrew Durbin, author of *MacArthur Park*

"A thrillingly imaginative zoological fantasia vivid with fierce intelligence, caustic observation, and sly humor. The concrete jungle has never felt so funny, so unexpected, and so wonderfully humane."
—Elan Mastai, author of *All Our Wrongs Today*

PRAISE FOR *DOUBLE TEENAGE*

"*Double Teenage* is a stunning first novel, moving
with stealth and intelligence against the
North American landscape."
—Chris Kraus, author of *I Love Dick*

"Joni Murphy's *Double Teenage* is a novel of shadowy
doubles, tracking the ghosts of adolescent girlhood between
America's "True West" and western civilization itself."
—Ariana Reines, author of Mercury and *The Cow*

"Murphy proves how deep youth is, how it sees with
exquisite senses honed especially pure for those whose
first landscape is the comparatively simple desert."
—Alisha Piercy, author of *Bunny and Shark*

FIRST CANADIAN EDITION

Talking Animals by Joni Murphy. Copyright © 2020 by Joni Murphy
Published by arrangement with FSG Originals, an imprint of Farrar,
Straus and Giroux.

Library and Archives Canada Cataloguing in Publication

Title: Talking animals / Joni Murphy.
Names: Murphy, Joni, 1980– author.
Description: First Canadian edition. | Originally published: New York:
Farrar, Straus and Giroux, 2020.
Identifiers: Canadiana (print) 20200285742 | Canadiana (ebook) 20200285874
    ISBN 9781771666053 (softcover) | ISBN 9781771666060 (EPUB)
    ISBN 9781771666077 (PDF) | ISBN 9781771666084 (Kindle)
Classification: LCC PS3613.U74 T35 2020 | DDC 813/.6—DC23

Printed in Canada

Book*hug Press acknowledges that the land on which we operate is the
traditional territory of many nations, including the Mississaugas of the
Credit, the Anishnabeg, the Chippawa, the Haudenosaunee and the Wendat
peoples. We recognize the enduring presence of many diverse First Nations,
Inuit, and Métis peoples and are grateful for the opportunity to meet and
work on this territory.

For the animals

In the dark times
Will there be singing?
There will be singing.
Of the dark times.

—Bertolt Brecht, *The Svendborg Poems*

"People come up to me and ask, 'Why are the
llamas humming?'" he said. "And I'll say, 'Because
they
don't know the words.'"

—Jennifer A. Kingson, "The Llama Is In,"
The New York Times, July 3, 2013

CONTENTS

THE FIVE BURROWS

I.

The city is an island and an island is a ship that never sails.

The city is a vessel for animals.

A long time ago, before the island was a city, it was a crumb of land bobbing in an ocean tea. But even then, it was jammed with plants and animals. The island has always teemed with life, moored as it is at a powerful juncture of rivers, the ocean, greater islands, and a whole roiling continent. It is hard now to picture the island of before, in its green state criss-crossed by streams and edged by marshes, as it has been changed so thoroughly by wave after wave of arrival and violence, construction and reconstruction. But before or after, this place was ever vital. This was never just any old island; it has always been a planet in miniature, a bubble of disordered life.

When the outsiders came they came in messy herds. Foreign birds arrived in flocks, and multitudes climbed from rough wooden crafts, all knees and heaves over the silty rocks.

Once grounded, some lay for a long time, crying for beloved friends lost at sea. Others put their grief aside and got straight to business. Whatever the attitude, all newcomers carried some memory, potent or cloudy, of the homes they'd left behind. They hoisted various flags and commenced the same battles that had driven them from their old lands in the first place.

More, then more arrived. You've never seen such a multitude. Everyone squeezed in and then did it again. So tight did it become that the ground in some areas disappeared beneath the crush of living creatures. The island swayed and creaked but did not sink because this was a ship of bedrock.

Native gulls turned above flocks of European starlings strategizing in trees.

The creatures from away brought with them panic. Gruesome histories trailed like a putrid smell. They had firm notions of how life should be lived, and they intended to impose them.

The island trembled.

Somebody cobbled a street where a soft path had been. Somebody drew a map. Somebody carried out a massacre.

Animals tore into one another. They spread diseases and infections. A pool of blood formed, dried up, then turned into flakes that the wind carried away. There is no story of a city that is not also a story of brutality. There is no story of brutality that has not been retold as one of heroism.

The invasive species began right away to mythologize themselves. They renamed everything. They got into fights with one another, and whoever won renamed places once again. They built houses, stores, bars, and jails out of the island's trees. The city burned again and again, and they rebuilt in whatever architectural fashion was current. Everything was brutal and everyone died. The living tore down old buildings and erected new ones in their place. They renamed streets and buildings after their dead, only for the living to die in turn.

To repress the psychic chaos that swirled inside, the living turned to numerology. They began to count everything and categorize what they'd counted. Someone measured out the whole island, then divided it with a grid. Grids sent the message that everything was under control. Meanwhile, more arrived and more died.

"Don't panic," they murmured to one another as they drew out long, straight lines.

Once they had the grid on their map, they set about filling every square on the real-life land. They built great halls and courthouses, they built fire stations and granaries. Around the edges they erected docks and strung bridges. Larger and larger ships kept bringing in more beings and things. Some grumbled because by now they saw themselves not as invasive, but rather as new kinds of native species. The community worked on complicated myths to explain away the violence at the core of their city-making.

Streets and avenues continued to creep, until they covered not just the first island but surrounding islands as well.

See! Here a beam, there a reservoir. Here a scaffold, there a retaining wall. Here a beer hall, there a bakery. Here a sweatshop, there an armoury. Here a train station with vaulted ceilings painted celestial blue, and there a system of grease-black tunnels.

The living paved over old cobbling. They numbered

and lettered the new trains. After vigorous debate, Helvetica was chosen as the official typeface for all signs. Buildings grew tall. Apartments stretched along streets like rows of stalls in a stable. Rooms proliferated inside like cells in a hive.

As the cityscape expanded, it also shrank. It came to feel as if the whole population lived together in one big house. Bricks, wallpaper, matted fur, insulation, granite, saliva, glue, venetian blinds, mud, twigs, vinyl siding, steel beams—they overlapped and merged. Architecture and infrastructure blurred into continuous surface. This great combine creased and flipped, so that private was public, and public concealed itself in plain view. Looking out might as well be looking in, as building walls made streets into halls. Foyers led to front doors, led to bedrooms with views of—if one was lucky—the Hudson River or the Kosciuszko Bridge.

In summer, sun pounded the sidewalks and the heat intensified the smell of everything. Citizens put plants into pots and put these pots on their sills. Youths leapt into turquoise pools that sat in the middle of emerald parks. Air conditioners hummed dangerously overhead. The city was like a pizza oven, and the inhabitants were greasy little toppings. These toppings felt weak or furious. Vendors sold chili mango and ices. Smoke and steam billowed up to join the clouds. The clouds grew tense. Rain fell heavy. The storm cleared up. Everyone felt happy, but then the heat would return, bringing with it fury and fatigue.

In late summer, places closed for vacation. Those who

could, fled. Then September would come, school would start, and everything would be open and packed once again.

Fall was the most beautiful.

Then came winter. The first snow was nice, but every subsequent just coated the frozen street filth. The mélange melted and refroze and the city would be miserable for months.

Winter lasted half a year or more before the winds blew in spring, when every tree exploded with pollen and flowers. Gingko and linden released their funky cream perfumes. The island went mad with joy and allergies.

The streets stank. Storefronts emitted puffs of salon chemicals and cooking grease, dung and bleach, fungus and air freshener. When crowds on the train pressed together they released whiffs of cocoa butter and Chanel.

Trash piled up. Workers took it away. There was so much stuff that even nice things cycled into the trash. Whoever got tired of their shoes just left them on the stoop. Someone else would put them on. Creatures threw out whole bedroom sets and decent abstract paintings. Socks, umbrellas, books, and incense could be bought on any street corner.

The crush, the wealth, the waste of wealth, all the tight quarters and inward-facing windows, made residents obsess over their bodies, their fur and feathers. They ignored seasonal dress and followed instead the gulf streams of fashion. Tatters in winter and suits for summer. Horn rims and corno portafortunas, buffalo plaids and leopard prints, socks and sandals—it all came and went, then returned later, reimagined. Everything was beautiful artifice.

Creatures obsessed over the unwritten laws of class, order, family, genus, and species. Mayors and council-members chattered among themselves, and with bankers. It had to do with ideology. It had to do with money.

The island, which was by now a city absolute, was full. One could get whatever one wanted, but walking around the block cost more than whatever you had in your pocket. A very few had way too much, some had enough, and many had nothing. Many moved away because they were tired, but plenty stayed because they didn't have enough to leave. Things got violent once again.

Though each age seemed as if it would go on indefinitely, the wheel of fortune turned. Outside wanted in afresh. Up wanted down. Those who'd fled to live in smaller herds drifted back to join the urban masses.

The bubble shifted and shimmered.

The city was a mystical chimera that spoke in the voices of multiple animals. It was a teacher, and its core lesson was that all must find peace with their own restless suffering. It also taught restlessness. The city didn't care who was jubilant and who was suicidal. It witnessed without comment. As a great teacher, the city had its true devotees, and they would twist themselves into knots to make sense of their master's riddles. They turned the incomprehensible into a logo, a slogan, a beast, a balloon in the parade. Pressure from within countered that from without in exquisite tension.

The city was an impossibility. An impossible yet existing place. It was a real piece of work. Animals from everywhere loved its whole routine. They adored the city enough to wear its name silk-screened on T-shirts. These shirts hailed others with a greeting that doubled as warning.

WELCOME TO NEW YORK, it read. NOW DUCK, MOTHERFUCKER.

UTOPIA OF RULES

2.

It was the start of some August Friday. The green-copper, brown-gold island gleamed. The park exhaled a cool sigh held from the night before.

Alfonzo Velloso Faca—student of urban behaviour, public servant, and brown, fluffy, big-eyed alpaca—emerged from the subway. He trotted along with the great flock of animals coming to Manhattan to make their dough. The crowd was large yet hushed. Everyone felt good because it wasn't humid for a change.

When the traffic lulled, Alfonzo dashed across Broadway and entered his favourite coffee shop, the Early Cenozoic. He hummed a few versions of a joke, and when it was his turn with the lemur barista he tried one out. She'd been working there since late spring but he had yet to establish a rapport.

"Did you hear the news?" he asked. "Some sea animals escaped from the aquarium."

"No! Did this just happen? Was it an uprising? Which aquarium?" The lemur clutched a mug, her eyes wide. Her machine hissed, temporarily forgotten. In the short line behind Alfonzo, a German shepherd was tapping her tail against the counter and a raccoon was fiddling with his newspaper.

Alfonzo had imagined more banter around the joke. He hadn't anticipated her seriousness. He stumbled. "I mean. It didn't happen in reality. I just— I heard it was otter chaos."

The music that had been playing reached its conclusion, leaving a silence for Alfonzo to squirm in. He felt like he'd shoved a used tissue into her paw. He watched the barista take his pun, turn it over and around in English until she saw what it was. "Oh. Utter like otter." Finally she bestowed upon him a slight nod, releasing them both from this snare of awkwardness.

Alfonzo added a wheat-grass cake he didn't really want to his coffee order and left a large tip as a mea culpa. Slinking toward the door, he heard the lemur apologizing to the shepherd for the wait.

These jokes were his hiccups. They came on without warning, spasmed through him, then departed. There was no repressing them, although his former fiancée, Vivi, insisted he could if he tried. Vivi said one should at least be *good* at punning if one had the indecency to say them aloud, and she even went further, suggesting that Alfonzo told bad jokes to humiliate himself because he was afraid of intimacy and craved judgment. Rather than responding to her comment, Alfonzo had searched for a good rhyme to pun with *intimacy: nutritionally, illiteracy, idiocy?* But Vivi's criticism returned to haunt him, at times like these, with its accuracy. He couldn't guess why he wanted to alienate the barista.

Alfonzo entered the park. It was 8:46 a.m. He had fourteen more minutes of freedom, and he could feel the building counting. City Hall knew the minutes and the seconds even for the most insignificant of its animal workers. Alfonzo thought of his dream from this morning and hummed the words *The End*. He had a pressing task to complete, but for the moment he wanted to let his thoughts float as he sipped his coffee. Taking a bench beside the central fountain, he basked in the sound of the water and in the yellow of the flowers. Shaggy green linden and thornless honey locust trees arched above. Beyond the trees towered Woolworths and the municipal building with its golden top. These old buildings dwarfed the trees just as the corporate towers dwarfed the old buildings. Traffic snaked along. The rhythmic mélange of sensations soothed, like a cool stream.

Baseball-hatted tourists milled around the park, oblivious to the space they took up as they waited for the morning tour of City Hall to begin. Workers darted around the clustered creatures as Alfonzo pondered and judged.

These tourists wanted, came for, and found another New York, a model city that existed within and yet separate from the one locals inhabited. These visitors came to pay full price at flagship department stores. They stopped by to wander MoMA at midday and scrunch their foreheads disapprovingly at the CoBrA retrospective. They seemed to enjoy waiting in long lines to eat mille feuilles served by feathery exchange-student wait staff. They shelled out big for tickets to musicals like *Laika* and *Bats in the Belfry.* They came to collect little anecdotes of Staten Island ferry rides and colourful characters. To become a tourist was to be rendered temporarily innocent.

The scurrying locals inhabited another layer. These two populations flowed along side by side, yet maintained a separation, like a rainbow of oil in a puddle.

To belong was taxing. It involved so much will and work. Alfonzo and everyone he knew was depleted. The locals were tired. They felt the constant need to show who they were or wanted to be with little symbols of significant affiliation or aspiration. Tote bags announced jobs at banks or time spent at an Ivy. A miniature flag stitched to a young goat's backpack told the world he was Dominican. According to their shirts, the pigeons at the breakfast cart were all union members from 32BJ SEIU. A pair of Siamese cats who emerged from an entryway touched noses before parting ways; if Alfonzo had to guess, he'd say they were executives. He based this on their purses. The city was an exhausting text that demanded endless reading.

Alfonzo saw in his mind's eye a poster, bought from a street vendor, of the Brooklyn Bridge. It hung in a black-and-white-tiled kitchen. He thought of the creature who'd taken the image. He thought of the ink suppliers, the print-shop worker, and the brotherhood of printer-repair animals who kept the machines working. He pictured the paper dust of all those images being made swirling into a storm that enveloped the whole city. He coughed.

The City Hall tour guide tromped down the steps to

lead the lost souls inside for the 9:00 a.m. tour. It was the cue Alfonzo wanted to ignore. He scanned the newspaper headlines to wring out a last moment of freedom.

MAYOR SHERGAR LOOSENS REGULATIONS FOR
  WATERFRONT DEVELOPMENT
PANEL URGES ACTION TO PROTECT FRAGILE ICE
  SHELVES; INDUSTRY OBJECTS
ABANDON BREEZY AFTER HURRICANE SPARKY?
  WATER-EVER, SAY LOCALS

That was a bad one, he thought with a snort. How many mechanisms must exist to turn tragedy into a digestible headline pun? His own plays on words were, he thought, harmless. But what were the puns of the news? These media makers were forming minds in this influential city. Some of the very creatures who oversaw this transformation had likely just passed before his judging eyes. Yet what right had he to judge? He was as much a part of the machine as anyone—scribbling and filing away. A humble cog, but still a cog. Alfonzo didn't joke because of intimacy, he joked because of fear and angst. He gathered his things and ambled inside.

How does an alpaca get to work on time?

Sheer force of wool.

3.

Alfonzo worked in the city's Department of Records, the shelf-lined memory folds of the civic brain. Building deeds; bids; city council minutes; birth, marriage, and death certificates; court notice and procurement decisions; survey photographs; weather charts; blueprints for libraries and park restrooms; tree maps; and sewer maps—all city documents that had ceased to be of active use were sent down to Alfonzo's department by way of an antique network of pneumatic tubes.

When he wanted to defend the department, he would say it was the foundation. When he was in despair, he would say he laboured in a grave.

The archive room—or rather chain of rooms—twisted through the ground beneath the white marble of City Hall. These underworld caverns had been dug by the noble badgers and moles of yesteryear.

The archive shelves were laid out in a grid. Regular files were stored in grey, acid-free boxes of uniform shape and colour, but some of these boxes held not files but smaller blue, red, and orange boxes. These in turn contained scraps of bark, skin, and other out-of-date writing surfaces. You couldn't tell from the outside which was which. You simply had to know.

Though the grid system appeared repetitive to the untrained eye, Alfonzo knew all the little details that delineated different neighbourhoods and moods within the larger structure. He could navigate by department name, year, content code, category and subcategory, and other basic shelving data, yes, but he also had a haptic sense of where things might be based on a mental map. There was the beige Chile-shaped water stain on the ceiling above the marriage records shelf. And off in the far corner of room 3, near last century's roadwork budget books, there was a mysterious cold draft with an accompanying spooky whistling noise.

Unique, precious, and historically important records were kept in a fireproof vault at a far corner of the deepest archive room. Even if the whole island were to go up in a great conflagration, the signature of the territories' first director general, Lord Corn; the speeches of the beaver mayor Nanfan St. Bernard; and that famous photo of city council speaker Niceto "Needles" Catanzarese, the trailblazing swine, would survive for future creatures to ignore.

Alfonzo's official title was second assistant to the commissioner of records. As second assistant, he had a series of unchanging tasks. One was to receive incoming documents, record said documents, and then file them in their proper locations. The pneumatic tubes wheezed before each new document arrived, that airy heave followed by an excremental plop as the envelope fell into the bag beneath the chute. That sequence sounded in Alfonzo's dreams.

In addition to tending paper, Alfonzo was in charge of recycling office materials, sweeping dust bunnies, and monitoring the humidity. The Department of Records was in a persistent battle with dampness, leaks, and mould. Those in City Hall who bothered to consider the combination of vital papers and subterranean damp knew that the department's location was far from ideal, but they knew just as well that moving the department was impossible, politically speaking.

It would be reasonable to assume that above Alfonzo there existed a first assistant, as well as a commissioner requiring assistance, but the positions were both vacant, and had been for some time. Alfonzo had been hired by Ketzel Tres Marias, the last commissioner of records. She pretended to be a nice raccoon grandma but was in reality a sharp-clawed operator. When Alfonzo started, a studious border collie named Lucky Saint Cloud was first assistant. Ketzel and Lucky did most of the challenging work and made Alfonzo handle the basic tasks they found too boring. But Alfonzo had just started grad school and was reeling from the collapse of his serious relationship with Vivi, so this arrangement had suited all of them. While Alfonzo moped and sorted, Ketzel could keep arguing about funding with the beasts upstairs and Lucky could run circles around the basement. He'd appreciated his two bosses, and they all worked in harmony for seasons.

The situation unravelled when Baldwin Shergar III was elected mayor.

Ketzel clashed with this new administration. She

became convinced they were trying to force her into early retirement. In her younger days, she might have schemed some subtle revenge, but she was in truth older, and fighting had become less appealing. Her husband wanted to move to Boca, she told Alfonzo with a sigh. "They don't have winter there." When it became clear Ketzel was going, Lucky might have used the opening as his chance to jump on top of the dog pile. But Alfonzo learned that Lucky harboured dreams of moving to the countryside. A short time after Ketzel announced her retirement, Lucky revealed he had accepted a job in the Buffalo library. Lucky told Alfonzo he had gotten into an intentional-living collective with a sheepdog couple, fifty sheep, three goats, and a flock of chickens. It sounded New Agey to Alfonzo, but he was happy for Lucky.

From then on, Alfonzo was alone. He thought replacement bosses would arrive, but they never did. It had something to do with the budget, the higher-ups said.

The vacancies, like the leaks and so many other problems, were always related to the budget. The budget was a practical and yet abstract creature invoked to explain away any and every issue within City Hall. Why do the subways run slow? Because the budget ate the money meant for a new signal system. Why must that hospital close? Because the budget got squeamish about the outer-borough ill.

Mayor Shergar had campaigned as a horse who would tame the budget. He snorted over pensions and promised that fat would be trimmed, departments streamlined and modernized and revamped. There would be public–

private partnerships, and he would shrink the budget from a tiger to a kitten, which would make it easier for the city to drown the budget in the river.

And yet, once Shergar took office, the budget only acquired new cravings. It wanted the mayor to throw soirées and give tax breaks as party favours. It sulked. The budget didn't want to expend too much of itself on the old or young, the infirm or the unruly. It wanted the attention of the rich and private. The budget had fantasies of omnipotence. It was hard to tell who, mayor or budget, was Svengali to whom.

The ins and outs of this relationship were of mostly casual interest to Alfonzo, but then he heard rumours that the mayor was planning to hire a private firm— Bunnywell Animals Atlantic—to take over public records.

When the city council opposed Shergar's plan and voted against the deal, Alfonzo sighed in relief. Though he did sometimes fantasize about getting fired, the voice of responsibility intruded on those daydreams to remind him of all the reasons he needed this steady job. *Without City Hall you'll slide into poverty, or you'll end up working at a wheat-grass shop and living with Luis in Ozone*, his fear wailed. So, he confined his dream to quitting only in order to become a professor. He crossed his toes and kept on filing and daydreaming.

Alfonzo continued working as the mayor and the council argued in chambers upstairs. The mayor retaliated by refusing to hire a commissioner of records or a first assistant. By leaving these two positions vacant,

Shergar drained the department of power without creating a spectacle. Few involved in the upstairs fight even knew the name of the second assistant. Alfonzo was a placeholder. As long as some warm body puttered in the basement, the records department was technically functional. Two unfilled positions in the labyrinth of city government was not news. All agreed to table the issue for an indefinite period. The foes moved on to arguing about lead in playground equipment. The budget whispered to the mayor about wasteful expense. The mayor wondered if lead was like iron; didn't doctors say iron was good for bones? Shergar's loyalists on the council suggested convening a panel of doctors to present the pros and cons of ingesting metals. The mayor approved.

Down in the basement, Alfonzo continued to wander in the fluorescent half-light. He skirted decomposing bankers boxes. He moved the standing fan around so that it blew on various wet spots on the floor. He persevered as the sole animal who knew the system's quirks, the tricks of the labyrinth that held the institutional memory of the city.

As was the dynamic, his best friend, Mitchell Cusco, who worked upstairs, tried to cheer him up. This anonymity was not a burden but a boon, and Alfonzo should cherish it. Think, Mitchell enthused, what Alfonzo could accomplish unwatched, unbothered, and surrounded by the rich history of the city. Use this opportunity to finish your dissertation, Mitchell cajoled.

Alfonzo was not just a worker, he was a stalled scholar who had been "all but dissertation" for a long while. ABD were his letters of shame. But it wasn't that he hadn't written a dissertation. Quite the opposite. It was that he had written too much of one.

The tale of Alfonzo the academic could be told in many ways. A cruel version might go: long-haired deadbeat pens left-wing trash while feeding at the public trough. The more charitable version could be: local kid makes good, juggles day job and night classes to honour the memory of his departed mother.

Alfonzo didn't know which version of himself rang truer. He was a left-wing-trash alpaca. He was the son of a local and an immigrant, and in this he fit some archetype. His father, Luis, was a quintessential outer-borough animal. He never left his borough and proclaimed that theirs was the best city in the world. Alfonzo's mother, Gina, had been born in the Andes. She and her parents had made the difficult journey from the Bolivian Altiplano to the city when she was very little. Both parents had been patriots and thinkers in their own ways. His mother, during her life, had venerated little things like getting the I VOTED sticker every few years. His father put great stock in home ownership. He felt that their home in Ozone Park was key to belonging. Luis had a square of grass of his own, and it was surrounded on all sides by layer upon layer of labour, immigration, history, and industry. Besides his lawn, Alfonzo's father put all his faith in the acquisition and maintenance of a public-sector job with a good pension. This outsized ego mixed with a strong desire for safety, Alfonzo thought, was very Queens.

Alfonzo wanted something different than his parents:

not status or land, but intellectual stimulation. He wanted to become Professor Velloso Faca, an intellectual powerhouse who laid bare class struggles and identity formation to undergrad flocks. He dreamed of writing incisive theoretical texts that managed to be both sophisticated and humorous. Alfonzo had devoted all these years to a dissertation that would tease out the myth of empire from the unwashed raw wool of reality. When he tried explaining this to Mitchell, his friend said it sounded muddled but brave.

Alfonzo's dissertation was a text dedicated to the struggles of *Vicugna pacos*, his species. And all that stood between him and a PhD was a conclusion he could not write.

That morning just before waking, Alfonzo had had a dream. The dream was of a single sheet of paper bearing the words *The End*. For some reason it was this that stirred him to action after so many seasons of floundering. He decided that today he was going to take a bold action. Humming a prayer to the clouds, Alfonzo slid a disk into his machine. He created a new page. This page he would slot in at the end of the text but before his nosenotes and footnotes. This was the page he'd been avoiding, but he was done procrastinating.

On the blank page he wrote the following:

Conclusion:
The End.

And that was it, a bold action. Alfonzo clicked send. Through wires the file moved from processer to printer.

The page emerged from the slot, and he checked it over. With that complete, he went back to the beginning. The rest of the text remained to be printed. He sent the full file TEXT.DIVERSION878 to the Aztek Howtek printer. The daisy wheel began to whir.

It was a long job and the machine was old, but he had a faith that came from his subconscious. Today was the day. He listened closely as the printer sputtered and coughed in a kind of mechanical throat-clearing. From the machine's grey slot, the first of his 1,532 pages slipped out. He was done being a cog. Now was the time for change. Alfonzo thrilled as he read his title arranged across the white page.

DISSERTATION

FROM ROAMING THE ALTIPLANO TO
SUPPLYING THE GARMENT DISTRICT: A
MOOKONIAN PSYCHOGEOGRAPHIC REVERIE
ON THE CAMELID DIASPORA OF THE NEW
YORK METROPOLITAN AREA

Submitted by Alfonzo Velloso Faca
Department of Pan-American Studies
In partial fulfillment of the requirements
for the degree of Doctor of Mammalian Philosophy
Hunter College
New York, New York

4.

Because his father hadn't been to college, let alone grad school, Alfonzo had a lot of anxiety and guilt. This difference between their experiences could curdle into resentment in the stomachs of both father and son. Luis sometimes called Alfonzo "Dr. Egg." Alfonzo sometimes snorted when his father mispronounced things and squirmed when Luis loud-talked to waitresses. Alfonzo wished to prove his father's way of life wrong but at the same time win his respect. He wanted to convince his whole family that intellectual work was *work*. And when it came to Hunter, Alfonzo wanted to show the fancier students he was quick enough to triumph in the perpetual fight of academia.

Alfonzo chafed at academic norms but still tried to behave right. The frisson of class resentment, the desire to understand and elucidate, kept him motivated for a long time. This clash of feeling had carried him through his formative years of fancy liberal arts undergrad and partway through his PhD. The scholarship to Hapshire had changed his life, and he was still struggling to realize the potential he supposedly had. It was at Hapshire that he'd met and fallen for Vivi, and there he'd been exposed to ideas and work that changed his brain chemistry, stomach flora, and sense of what was possible.

But this energy had dissipated. His mother had died after he completed his comps, and the old motivating anger turned to amorphous grief. Who was he mad at? The metaphorical father was the easy answer, but his real father had turned grey and frail. Alfonzo found he couldn't stay furious with a widower alpaca whose wool hung around his body like a thin layer of melancholic smoke.

When he'd first accepted his job at City Hall, Alfonzo told himself that he was smarter than his grad school peers with their loans and free time. Though it would take longer to complete his degree, eventually he would emerge from his cocoon as a fluttering professor-monarch with understanding of both the public sector and academia. He was no slouch.

But the fact was, he envied his classmates. They finished their degrees, while he plodded behind. He was jealous of those who went to summer programs and on research trips. But he was also furious that his school favoured the more privileged in so many large and small ways, while at the same time presenting itself as a bastion of lefty, emancipatory values. When he grew tired of the trap, Alfonzo would look away from school toward his childhood friends. He felt jealous of their relaxed states, their badly-thought-out politics. They seemed to be able to just enjoy the kind of life he'd trained himself to ruthlessly deconstruct.

He could rage at the classist snobbery of the university using discourse he'd acquired there. This erudite grumbling did nothing productive. His school colleagues thought him bitter; his old friends thought him a snob. Neither group was really wrong. He hated the shape he'd taken on. To cope, Alfonzo had put his head down and worked. And this was how he had come to produce a 1,532-page-long dissertation.

In writing and reading, Alfonzo chewed on anything that had even a vague connection to camelid identity. He learned about the social, political, and mystical histories of the Andes. He pored over guinea pig oral histories. He entertained the kooky artiodactyl theory that camelids were all distant relatives of dolphins and whales. He pondered the symbolic significance of toes and stomachs, and the absence or "lack" of humps. He wrestled with arguments that spitting was a form of ritual rather than a violent act. He meditated on images of sand, water, and mountains. Translational nuances, phenomenological asides, footnotes on hooves—there was no academic flourish Alfonzo eschewed. His text rippled outward in ever-expanding concentric arguments.

When friends made the mistake of asking about the subject of his dissertation, he would hum, then ask them softly, "What is anything about? What is animal life about?"

And his friends would puzzle. "Are you high?" they would query.

He'd borrow one of his dad's nonsensical quips: "As high as a flea on the underdog."

Why was his dissertation 1,532 pages long? Because it was about all alpaca life. No, but why, really?

Because he was afraid of ending.

Viviana was right, he craved failure. Alfonzo was bitter and confused because he could see that the text he'd written had no end. The academy wanted him to conclude, and he wanted to keep unspooling.

He knew he should edit, but he couldn't bring himself to do it. Each chapter leaned on another, and all bore weight. Was he supposed to choose between chapter 3, "Cloud and Astral Llamas," and chapter 7, "On Forced Labour in the Guano Mines"? Or should he cut chapter 19 on camelid solidarity with Guatemalan donkey guerrillas to make room for chapter 30, "Wool Work and Woolworth: Alpacas' Five-and-Dime"? Obviously, the chapter on how camelids became "mammals" in the eyes of the establishment was as necessary as, if not more so than, "Alpaca Red, Alpaca Blue: Labour Activism and Law Enforcement." And then of course there were the sentimental chapters, like the autobiographical one on music and subculture. For "From Jaguarondi Cumbia to Los Crudos: Popular Music as a Window into the Shifting Politics of Three Generations," he'd done a deep study of his grandparents' and his parents' record collections and contrasted them with his own aesthetic leanings. He couldn't take a scalpel to this tribute to his grandmother and mother.

More, Alfonzo couldn't admit to his will to fail. He had better and more comfortable coping mechanisms to fall back on. He preferred critiquing the institution itself to critiquing his own work. Academia was just another predatory con game, was it not? And he was just another mark. A brick down somewhere toward the bottom of the great pyramid.

Outsiders dismiss scholars as bloodless obscurants. Those inside the walls know, though, that every scholar fights for or against *something*. Teeth are bared. Some fight to correct an old, oppressive, official narrative, while others quarrel to protect their scrap of field. Academia is a dangerous landscape in which all inhabitants are forever preparing themselves to be seen and chosen. Everyone draws a boundary, they pee around the edges of their turf. But what is enclosed within the disciplinary hedges? Who are the foxes? Who are the hounds? Who trims the topiary? Who owns this land? Is nothing common?

Alfonzo knew he had lost his way. Whichever path he took, he became immediately disoriented. The dissertation had become his Everest—or, to use a more appropriate South American reference, his Aconcagua. Yes, that faraway mountain was the perfect analogy for his sea-level struggle. Alfonzo felt like he was dying from lack of oxygen. He was simultaneously too high and too low.

The Aztek Howtek printer clicked as it rolled out page 237 of Alfonzo's dissertation. He trotted around the office, filing the day's files while listening to the comforting mechanical spit of the printer.

Barring mishap, the dissertation would be ready before lunch. He planned to slip out at four and rush to Hunter. American Studies closed at five, and today was the deadline for dissertation submission. He was hoping for the real possibility that his adviser would not read all the way through and his abrupt ending would go unnoticed.

The printer continued whirring out pages. Alfonzo wandered deeper into the files.

Since the loss of Ketzel and Lucky, the Aztek Howtek printer had become Alfonzo's de facto confidant. The printer was a grey relic and about the size of a chopping block. It exhibited a subtle sentience to him, and Alfonzo had come to care for the machine. The maintenance animals had long ago stopped servicing it. Alfonzo expected they'd forgotten. Despite its age and neglect, the Aztek Howtek persisted. It was a survivor. It continued to live and work in obscurity. It did not judge or comment, aside from its geriatric wheezes and squeaks.

Alfonzo had leaned on the Aztek Howtek countless times over the years, and the printer had marked different milestones. Alfonzo had printed copies of impossible-to-obtain texts, such as a whole bootleg copy of *Browsing as Method and Itchy Subjects: Who Are the Fleas in the Political Fur?* Alfonzo had printed the first article he'd ever gotten published, "Equine Realism: Is There No Alternative?," on this machine.

The printer insisted on a few simple yet inflexible rules. It didn't staple, or use any size of paper aside from eight-and-a-half-by-eleven. It did not collate. Wrinkles gave it fits. The Aztek Howtek communicated only with Alfonzo's word processor, and accepted one job at a time. You sent a new job before the previous had finished at the peril of losing everything. If any of the Aztek

Howtek's preferences were ignored, it let out a squeal until Alfonzo came to wrestle out the hot crimped-up mess from the inner cylinders.

What the Aztek wanted was simplicity and a steady diet of paper and black toner. Alfonzo treated the machine like a demented grandfather who had once been a skilled worker. And because Alfonzo was good about providing for it, he'd come to assume he and the printer were on the same side.

"But of course, assuming makes an *ass* out of *you* and *me*," Alfonzo's father liked to say. To which Alfonzo would retort, "Wouldn't it make an ass out of *u* and *ming*?"

"If you used half the smarts you use mouthing off to do your job, you'd be mayor by now," Luis would grumble.

"I'd rather be dead."

Since Alfonzo's mom had died, he and his father had been trying to be kinder with each other. Voicing a desire for suicide was as gentle as they could muster.

Alfonzo was scanning a shelf while having an imaginary fight with his father when the beeping began.

His father believed Alfonzo was unlucky in a metaphysical sense—a trait he associated, for some reason, with Alfonzo's curly wool. His father kept track of all Alfonzo's ordinary hiccups of fortune and assembled these into evidence of a mystical, preordained ill fortune. When Alfonzo heard the beeping, he felt the truth of this in his very follicles.

The Aztek Howtek was emitting a series of bad beeps.

His various stomachs tied themselves in various knots.

Through the pneumatic tubes, he thought he could hear the faint cackle of the creature called Budget.

5.

Most workers rely on magic, astrology, and prayer when it comes to appeasing their office appliances. Of course, there are those maintenance creatures who truly understand the inner wheels of a printer, those who know the codes and the wires, but for most, electrical machines run on sorcery.

Murphy's Law is cosmic office truth. "Whatever can go wrong, will go wrong" is one formulation, but it could be restated as follows: "Nature always sides with the hidden flaw." Whatever has gone right in the past will go wrong when it matters most. Or, put yet another way, just when you think you've got a system, the system has got you. These mysterious machines will betray you, not out of malevolence, but because you have not learned to behave by their rules or see their intrinsic nature.

Alfonzo was trying to force the printer to act based on a zoomorphic understanding. He thought of the printer as a fellow animal who ate paper and drank ink. He had told himself a story in which the printer was, like him, a bored basement-dweller hungry for plant matter.

Alfonzo ransacked drawers and shelves for blank paper. And every ten seconds the machine beeped.

Alfonzo paced around his basement. He sighed and twitched. He stared at the Aztek Howtek printer and sighed again. He studied the already printed portion of his dissertation, the first 786 pages. He hummed to himself, *Calm down, wool for brains.* But how could he? He had no more paper.

There was a lump of wheat-grass cake from breakfast in Alfonzo's left cheek and he was working it hard. The fresh chlorophyll had gone, and all that was left was a stringy, cardboard-tasting mass. Not that he minded; chewing helped with his anxiety. A Black Cat brand ciggie would have helped more, but he'd quit. *No,* he hummed to himself, *smoking is bad.* Ugh.

Alpacas are habit-prone animals. Humming and chewing were the two habits most common to their kind. Birthright traits entwined with the deep identity of all camelids. Alfonzo had written two chapters—both now caught in the limbo between processor and printer—on the practical and psychic significance of humming and chewing. In a way, humming was straightforward, a dialect, a mode of communication that turned in toward the organs and out toward the Other. It was a way to work through stresses and questions. It was also the way camelids communicated among themselves when they wanted to be private. Humming was untranslatable. In the community, it served as quotidian telepathy. Other animals couldn't understand, just as camelids couldn't understand the chatter of other species. Dogs had dog tongue—or conversation with scent and saliva—just as birds had bird speak, and rabbits had whatever anxious chatter they had.

It was impolite to probe into the private communication systems of others.

Chewing, in contrast, was complicated and more brutish. To chew was to be judged. Yet camelids weren't the only chewers, or even spitters for that matter. And chewing was, like humming, both soothing and nourishing; it likewise filled odd moments and provided something to do during nervous ones. Chewing cut across alpaca/llama society and connected with larger political, emotional, and social issues. Chewing was a hallmark of the entire ruminant community, and the ruminant matrix was complex.

The most famous and influential ruminants were, of course, cows, but the wider classification included many. Alpacas, llamas, vicuñas, sheep, goats, and moose were all united by their multiple stomachs and love of vegetarian restaurants.

Ruminants were frequently mocked by the socially dominant single-stomached. Cats, dogs, horses, pigs, and raccoons were all too comfortable making cracks about grass-bag bellies, about burps and endless chawing. A whole hygiene and supplement industry had arisen to "solve" what was deemed a shameful digestive problem.

Ruminant intellectuals had developed whole philosophies based around the digestion question. Alimentary deconstructionists envisioned stomach as mind and food as information. They held that beauty and complexity arose from slow digestion. Charlene Mooken had devoted her career to the subject. She wrote that gut and mind were inseparable, that the pockets and folds of the brain were mirrored in the digestive tract. Ruminants, she argued, had been instrumental in the development of animal society because of—not despite—their slowness to digest.

Once, Alfonzo had made the error of explaining epistemological folds to his father. He'd regretted it. After that instance of intellectual sharing, his dad had brought up a twisted-up version of Alfonzo's summary to bolster his own problematic speciesist arguments.

"You can't generalize, Dad! Not all those with one stomach are idiots."

"Well, your French cow girlfriend thinks they are."

"She's a dead philosopher, not my girlfriend."

"Potato *tomato*," his father had huffed.

Each replay of this argument reminded Alfonzo of the perils of getting into alpine philosophy with family.

In his own life, Alfonzo tried to develop his own propensity for slowness into a radical position. He chewed on his thoughts like they were grass, and on grass like each blade was a word in a sentence. He would hum *no*, while also seeing arguments for *always already* and *yes and*. Why did he need to choose? He would turn over the possibility that truth might be a perpetual flicker. Perhaps one needed to hold complexity always in one's stomach. Truths, he thought, must lie somewhere amid endless questions, self-recriminations, excuses. Like pebbles scattered throughout a brambled field. Some might call the ruminants a species of flip-floppers. But Alfonzo preferred to think of his kind as organically rhizomatic thinkers. His dad scoffed whenever Alfonzo used words like *rhizomatic*.

But stop, he hummed to himself. *Focus, hay-head.* This wasn't about his father. This wasn't about digestion. This moment was about paper. The printer needed paper, or it needed to be unplugged. Those were the two options. Neither was good.

Alfonzo chewed his tasteless grass ball. The machine bleated.

If he unplugged the machine, the printer would be silent. It was tempting. But unplugging Aztek Howtek would also erase the machine's memory. It would forget everything, what page it was on, if it did or did not have ink. The machine might very well have an existential crisis and fall into an hours-long fugue state. Unplugging was a desperate act.

Alfonzo's ears wiggled as though they were trying to flick away the sonic flies of the printer's complaints. He felt like ramming into the wall. His big dumb ears would protect his brain from damage.

The Aztek Howtek bleeped.

Alfonzo cursed luck, planning, the university system, and his overall approach to life.

The bleating continued.

If a machine runs out of paper in a basement, and only a second assistant hears it, does it make a sound? Yes, Alfonzo could answer that koan.

Mitchell, the tall and talented llama who always solved Alfonzo's problems, was in his own office right upstairs. Alfonzo didn't want to go running to him yet again, but his friend would have a clue—or paper.

6.

Mitchell Cusco—lifelong pal of Alfonzo Velloso Faca and the public sector's most handsome and popular llama—was not actually in his office. Rather, he was watching currents of animal ebb and flow across the park. It was 11:17 a.m., and Mitchell had been on a "site visit" all morning. That site had been his straw bed, but no one in the Hall needed to know that.

Sheepy clouds and blue skies reflected in the skyscrapers' glass. The mirroring made the buildings almost invisible. Black cars and buses grumbled at lights. Delivery birds flitted above traffic. A pack of teenage raccoons yelped and tussled. Some breakdancing goats jumped around for cheering tourists. The fountain waters flew in an arch.

Last night had been a late one. Mitchell was faded around the edges. Luckily, he had neither meetings nor any immediate deadlines. His various supervisors were on vacation.

Mitchell's plan for what remained of the morning was simple. He would get a coffee or something so that he might be able to flirt with Pamella, the lemur barista, and then retreat into the cool embrace of his office to ruminate on a couple of ibuprofens. He would then spend a few hours reviewing building code violation forms while listening to Spike and the Mad Dog bicker over the finer points of the Orioles' coaching strategy.

Mitchell stretched, then bopped across Broadway to visit the loveliest barista in all of Manhattan. "Oh, Pamella," he hummed. "How you've rearranged me."

The Early Cenozoic had been recently redecorated. Vintage illustrations of coffee plants and terraced tea plantations hung on brick walls. The landlords were trying to attract more customers, Mitchell supposed. Not that they needed to. Their big front window faced City Hall. All the bureaucrats had to go there if they wanted decent caffeine. Not that every pen-pusher cared about *decent*. There was no accounting for taste.

Pamella was behind the register, staring into space with her perfect circle eyes. When Mitchell came in, she acknowledged him with a blink. He felt that this meant something. She didn't blink at everyone that way. They had a complex understanding.

"Your face is a tuft of amber delight."

She blinked again.

"The thought of you helps me survive the long hours in my dim office prison," Mitchell continued. "You can't imagine how they have us packed in. Like sardines in a tin. The thought of you keeps me going."

"Oh, stop." Pamella plucked a leaf from a sad little potted plant on the counter and popped it in her mouth. "Don't tell the bosses I'm eating the decor."

"Never."

"What will you have, Mitchell?"

Mitchell had been waging a subtle though as-yet-unsuccessful campaign to get the café to branch out into drinks more exotic than the usual coffee and tea. What wasn't on their menu had become a subject of banter between him and Pamella. He would conjure something unusual, and she would dismiss his request. The birds who owned the place were conservative in their bulk orders. Therefore, Mitchell already had a cheek full of some guayusa he'd ordered all the way from Ecuador. All he really needed was hot water, which he could get in his office. But office water would not grant him visions of Pamella.

"Could I just get a cup of hot water?"

"I'll have to charge."

"For hot water?"

"They count the cups," she grumbled.

"Would they charge for cold?"

"Plastic water cups are free."

Not wanting to get her in trouble, he took out some money. He slid it, she slid it back. He returned it, and she gave in and sucked her teeth and thanked him.

"So, you're drinking plain hot water? You're crazy, boy."

He showed her his ball of leaves in reply.

"Oh, I see," she purred. "Secret herbs."

"You know, my friend Al probably needs a little pick-me-up. I'll take a green drink for him, actually."

Mitchell wondered if Alfonzo knew Pamella's name.

The two friends hadn't spoken of her, and Mitchell had yet to disclose his crush.

Though Pamella knew most everyone from the Hall by sight, many of his colleagues treated her as close to invisible. She was just another part of the service mechanism, like a door handle or a cup. Mitchell knew it was their loss, because Pamella was a radical, an intellectual, and a true inspiration. Through their casual banter, she'd turned Mitchell on to all sorts of new ideas. He longed to take her on a proper date, but was as yet too nervous to ask. He bided his time, read her pamphlets, and prepared arguments in favour of ginseng tonics and chicory foam.

Pamella twitched her furry doughnut-hole ears. As she gave him the drinks, she slipped alongside a little blue booklet. Mitchell took the pamphlet and hid it in his pocket, then blinked at her, five times slowly. They understood each other.

"Would you mind," she asked, "sharing a smidge of your herb?"

Mitchell was surprised. Sharing saliva, even apart from kissing, felt intimate. He separated a lemur-sized bite of the wet herb and spit it delicately onto a napkin.

"You're a peach," said Pamella.

"See you," he sighed.

"And the sea sees you," she replied.

Once safely back in his first-floor office, Mitchell let his mind drift. His nerves buzzed and sparked as he watched the dark shapes of his colleagues swim by the frosted glass of his office door. Hooves and heels clicked, claws skittered, toe pads whispered along the cool floor.

City Hall was much too small a building for the metropolis it represented. It had been erected for another city—a smaller, more feral one, where beavers and dogs roamed the muddy streets trading bits of wood and flesh for tobacco and metal. They—whoever the old *they* was—should have razed or renovated the original building to better fit with the outsized city, but the state loves the European messages contained in cupolas, ornamental swags, and Corinthian columns. *They* weren't going to destroy this symbol for anything.

Because of this allegiance to old animals, the current animals had to fight for space. Many departments were crammed together along each corridor and on each floor, and everyone wanted to be as close to the mayor as possible. Which floor you were located on communicated a lot about your political status. The least glamorous departments—Water, Sanitation, and his friend Alfonzo's own ignominious Records—were located in the leaky, fungal basement. The mayor's suite was on the third floor. Mitchell's "office" had once been a utility closet and had neither heat nor ventilation—but it was private, had gold letters on the door, and was located on the respectable first floor. He was quietly proud.

Mitchell had devoted much effort to acquiring a space for himself. Getting it required a lot of complimenting and joking around with the right animals. A private office was how Mitchell kept his sanity. But maybe it was also how he'd lost his mind. Sucking up to and keeping track of a bunch of bureaucracy jackasses had taken its toll. He had to keep his friends close, or in the basement anyway, but a few fucking asshole idiots closer—down the hall.

Mitchell excelled in subtle bureaucratic games because he'd been taught by the best, his uncle Ernesto Cusco Llama. Uncle Ernie was one of those creatures who embodied the folk tale of social mobility. He'd begun life as night watch at a cat food factory, only to work his way into the more feral world of local government. He was the first llama in history to become a city councillor. A small plaque in a weedy triangle "park" near District 28 commemorated the fact.

It would be a lie to say that having an insider uncle hadn't helped Mitchell. Ernie had convinced him to take this path in the first place. He'd extolled the values of public service at every holiday and family get-together. While Ernie took pains to avoid blatant nepotism, he wasn't shy about bringing his nephew into the fold once Mitchell got the job. One could argue that shepherding family into one's profession was the very definition of nepotism, but it was also how the system worked. "Just hum it off," advised Ernesto, "and go about your business."

This initial nepotistic boost didn't mean that Mitchell's job title was anything fancy. His uncle had died a while back, and no one in the Hall from the old days was still around. Whatever influence that had been had dissolved into dust and long ago been swept up. Mitchell was just a working llama schmo, just the junior administrator of management under the umbrella of the greater Housing

Authority office. Most of his work involved fielding the inquiries of the angry, the troubled, or the disappointed. He spent a great deal of time putting animals on waiting lists and sending threatening letters to landlords who were trying their best to circumvent regulations. In practical terms, this meant that Mitchell dealt with many animals close to homelessness and another group of animals who were trying to take away those homes.

In many ways it was a depressing post, but Mitchell enjoyed the fight. He savoured winning small victories and sticking it to the powerful and their toadies. He was hopeful by nature. Mitchell was—philosophically speaking—an animalist, if a practical one. He believed in lofty but not transcendental animal ethics. He and Alfonzo often argued about the nature of justice. Alfonzo was more pessimistic. But Mitchell had believed life was arcing toward a unity of animal togetherness. It was just taking a while.

Lately, though, something within him had become unsettled. Pamella had been telling him about the sea, and its battered communities. She'd opened his eyes to a long history of brilliant creatures, hunted and speared and ground into cat food. There had never been a whisper about this in school. Her narrative of the world reversed the world he'd known. He'd been reading her pamphlets and brooding about politics. He hummed and thought of Pamella. She'd disturbed something.

———

From down the hall came the tippy trot of Mr. Leonard "Lenny" Old Spots.

Mitchell sighed. Reverie broken.

The pig was director of the mayor's Office of Operations. This powerful-because-vague position gave him an excuse to drop in on various animals whenever he wanted. If the job title fell below his, and most did, Lenny Old Spots could ask anything, all in the name of efficiency. He was always gathering or double-checking. Everyone knew the pig had the mayor's ear, so it was dangerous to resist him. Old Spots was a gossip, basically an officially appointed spy.

Lenny Old Spots embodied a movie-inflected concept of a real New Yorker: loud and heavy with accent, smart yet thick, and jokey-mean. He lived in White Plains, which Mitchell hardly considered the city. He had season tickets to the Mets. He was at the top of his salary scale and would retire with tier-one benefits. After a heart attack, the pig was given a baboon heart. He called animals he considered weak either "honey" or "boss." He often referred to himself as a "proud porcine American" and railed against the historic oppression of his kind. "We are prey, too," he would volunteer if he ever heard a squirrel or rabbit discussing their fear of violence.

There was a group of animals in City Hall, among them Mitchell's friend Dawn Delamarche, a deer in the Department of Education, who found Old Spots charming. This love of the pig drove Mitchell wild, but he found it difficult to protest without coming across like a jerk.

"He's harmless!" Dawn would say. "It's just his generation."

Authenticity was a favourite fetish of many suburban transplants like Dawn, and the pig performed it better than someone like Mitchell or Alfonzo or anyone else who'd struggled to shed their outer-borough coat. Little did they know when they were young that their high-school-bully aesthetics would be all the rage with liberal arts chicks when they reached adulthood. Dawn pined for the old East Village, the bygone Lower East Side. She waxed nostalgic about the loft she used to have on Myrtle Avenue back in her art education days, when that street still carried a whiff of predators.

Suburban animals like Dawn marked the time of their arrival to New York as just the time when the city was still gritty enough, wild enough; when Avenues A, B, C, and D still meant adventurous, brave, crazy, and dead, rather than what they had become: agreeable, blah, characterless, and dull. Characters like Lenny Old Spots performed a New Yorkness they recognized from the media. So they loved him.

"Being from New York is not a personality," Mitchell would yell.

Alfonzo would agree and try to calm him. It was an epidemic.

Their friend Dagoberto had developed a Brooklyn-esque accent that would have made his great-grandparents flinch. It was too embarrassing to ask why he talked like a turn-of-the-century rag seller when he was in reality a present-day graphic designer.

Lenny Old Spots was not charming. He was a type. An outer-borough porker without shame who, rather than toning himself down, grew more aggressive as the times changed around him. He said shitty things in his antiquated accent.

In many ways the whole city had been deformed by the disastrous influence of a similar such pig, former mayor Napoleon Herbert. The violence, corruption, and unrest of that period had had far-reaching consequences. That pig's influence had been so damaging that elements of the city charter were rewritten to guard against anyone like him ever taking control again. Many pigs still carried a feeling of collective guilt and shame when it came to Herbert. It had taken much work on the part of the pig community to repair relations with their fellow creatures. Many pigs were quite polite and self-effacing, still apologetic after so many generations, even though the living pigs couldn't be held responsible for the violence of their ancestors.

But there were others, like Old Spots, who went out of their way to be insufferable assholes. Or perhaps, in the case of Old Spots, being an asshole just came naturally.

The pig pushed the door open. "You busy?"

"Yes . . ."

"Oh, good."

"No, I mean, I was . . ." *Hum.* There was no point in fighting it. This interaction was under the pig's control. "So, what can I do for you today, Lenny?"

"My buddy heard there's a big building development in the works, and that there might be some protests or something. I wondered if you, as a fellow swimmer, knew anything."

"I haven't heard."

"I thought you were friends with the waves."

"I don't know what you're talking about."

"Sure you don't." The pig winked, mimicked blowing bubbles. "Blub blub blub."

Old Spots was a bit anti-llama. The pig also held a dim view of birds, was squirrel skeptical, critical of both cats and rabbits, and openly anti-rat. Well, he was anti-everyone. Though Mitchell tried to push back, it wasn't about making sense. "But, Lenny," he would say, "goats have lived everywhere—they're in Europe, they're in the Americas, in Asia; they're so ancient they're on the zodiac."

"Exactly," the pig would squeal. "The zodiac! All those shifty zodiac animals. Thank you. Thanks for making my point for me."

That was the kind of logic Mitchell had to contend with. Comparatively, though, it was nothing. This generalized bias against the animals he lived among was practically love compared to Old Spots's feelings about the ocean.

Mitchell tried to stay polite. "Is that all?"

It never was, with Old Spots.

"I heard the building is going to be made out of reflective glass so that no one can see inside. It won't have floors, but they'll make it seem like it does."

Mitchell couldn't stop himself. "How would that even work?"

"From outside, the building will appear normal. It'll have a doorlike rectangle in front, and what appears to be different levels going up and up, but all that's a false front. Inside will be its true structure. If you know what I mean."

"I don't."

"Picture a hollow glass tube. A skyscraper beaker. At the bottom there will be a giant valve connecting the building to the sewers, and through the sewers, to the ocean. And one day, when conditions are right, the cabal will open the valve and sea water will rush in and fill the tower all the way to the top. That's how they'll take us over."

"And who's behind this construction?" Mitchell asked.

"Elite seals."

"Lenny, have you ever talked to an engineer in your whole life? Factually I know you have, but based on that explanation it's as if you have no idea about infrastructure, architecture, or sea animals. Reality is not a system of tubes."

"You dromedaries are content to ignore the threat. But when the waters have risen up to your neck, you'll be kicking yourself, Mitchell."

"I'll be too busy dog-paddling to kick myself."

Old Spots had gotten riled. "Listen, fur-ass. I'm telling you the sea is coming for the city. I know animals in construction, and a huge tank is feasible. I know what I know."

Mitchell felt compelled to wind the pig up a twist

more. "This is neither here nor there, but dromedaries are camels, and I'm, I mean, we're related to camels, but . . ."

The pig wasn't listening.

"Never mind. What position do you think I should be taking about floorless buildings?"

Old Spots glanced down the hall before closing the door behind him. He enjoyed behaving as if life were a thriller. "Now, I know you and I don't always see eye to eye, but I think, as land animals who work for the state, and as just, well, *honourable* animals, we've got to protect our kind. I've been hearing that rents are rising because developers are investing in these luxury tank projects. They're hiding the sea all around us. It's a plot."

Since the hurricane, many land animals had taken to blaming the sea for every woe. They complained about waves and storms. The *Post* found ways to link the seas to everything from avian flu to volcanic eruptions. If you listened to right-wing radio, the sea was somehow the source of fleas and mange, mould and bad dreams. There were all sorts of crazy conspiracies.

Old Spots was convinced that there was a secret sea organization bent on destroying first New York, then eventually all dry land. He believed that various land mammals were in collusion with a cabal of whales, dolphins, and seals working to annihilate everything he loved. Whenever he wanted to criticize some cat, goat, or bird, he insinuated that they were an agent of the sea. Mitchell could not convince the pig that this was a bigoted idea.

"But oceans already cover seventy per cent of the Earth."

"Those extremists won't be happy until they've gotten it all."

"How do you think they're going to 'attack'?"

"Excuse me, did you forget Hurricane Sparky?"

"That was a natural disaster."

Old Spots snorted. "It's those extremist SERFs," he said—the Sea Equality Revolutionary Front. "They're planning to flood the subways and the sewers, forcing us to swim like rats."

"Why would sea creatures even want that?"

"They hate our legs and our free society."

"*Hum?*"

"It's all connected, see? They want us all drowned. These buildings don't have any floors because . . ." Old Spots paused for emphasis. "They're huge aquariums full of fanatical sea creatures. When you and I are walking down the street, we're being watched by sharks and stingrays and whales and those fucking dolphins. They're right there plotting our demise while we go about our business, like suckers!"

Mitchell laughed and Old Spots frowned. The sad thing was that the reality of New York real estate was already so fantastical that anything felt plausible. More and   more development had less and less to do with need. There was already a complex designed to look like a forty-storey pair of pants. There was another everyone called the Swiss cheese block. Another building was designed like a tall,

66

narrow zero, hollow in the middle. In this landscape of architects' follies, an aquarium tower didn't sound that outrageous.

Mitchell pictured this cartoon building. A supertall high-rise where dolphins darted up toward the rooftop surface to servant creatures who sprinkled expensive fish food.

The pig barrelled on. "Now imagine if one of these slick maniacs decides to pull the plug or break a hole in the wall of their watery tower. Boom. Downtown Tribeca, flooded. Central Park, a wetland. Thousands drowned. Pandemonium."

"A little extreme, no?"

Old Spots snorted. "It's our job to imagine worst-case scenarios. You have to think like those gutterpups. You may like to believe that you're here to prop up some nanny-goat-state nonsense, but I want you on my side, because when we're all dog-paddling for our lives it won't be about rich versus poor, it will be about legs versus fins."

"Umm . . ."

"Look, boss, no offence, but in my position, I may be privy to some intel you don't get down here in Housing." The pig smirked.

Mitchell hated him.

It wasn't that Old Spots was stupid. It wasn't even that there was nothing to worry over. Mitchell could see that the city was crumbling and the oceans were seething. It was that Old Spots transformed questions into a cudgel. He only wanted to see the most fragile punished. The pig was blaming the world's problems on fish, when fish were getting poisoned and eaten, and eaten and poisoned, by all the creatures on land who'd built their industries on sea exploitation. The pig was right and wrong in Mitchell's eyes, and yet they could only communicate across a chasm of difference. What was being shared? Mitchell didn't know. Everything got twisted.

How can you be so naive? they wondered at each other.

"I'm sharing this with you because I think you're not a complete nose bag," Old Spots offered.

"Your faith is inspiring."

"I'm trying to get your head in the game, Mitch."

There was a knock. Old Spots turned to the interloper. "What's shaking, Shaggy."

"Pardon?" Alfonzo said.

"Be good, chief." And with that the pig departed.

"Thanks for stopping by, Leonard!" Mitchell called out.

"Should I be offended?" Alfonzo asked his friend. "I'm confused."

"Oh, buddy, you saved me," Mitchell hummed.

7.

Alfonzo slumped into Mitchell's office. "I'm in trouble."

"Your haircut?"

"Be. Nice."

"Not to take the pig's side, but he does have a point."

"Brother, don't."

"I mean, I'm no barber, but I could take a whack."

It was Mitchell's philosophy that friends should tease each other about trivial foibles but then also fight to the death to protect each other from real external threats. The herd was sacred, but within the group there was a nice, consistent padding of emotionally distancing banter—that was his style.

"Remember when you sold your wool to pay for textbooks?"

"Thank you for bringing up a humiliating moment. You know you could have talked me out of it."

"Whatever, it grew back and your baldness provided months of comedy."

"I'm glad my poverty was so funny. But I didn't come to rehash the history of my grooming."

They tapped this vein of banter often. Another precept of Mitchell's philosophy of friendship was that one must revel in repetition. Everyone was repetitive. The longer you knew someone, the more times you had to listen to him sing his hit songs. Everyone had a finite repertoire. Some friends sang of heartbreak, others of aggravation. Sometimes you sang together, other times you listened to them solo. That was conversation. Alfonzo's core sonic theme was self-recrimination. He had the habit of letting any one moment of disappointment become an opportunity to tally all shortcomings. One snappy chorus went something like "I'm a failure and this is a disaster." Mitchell knew all his friend's songs by heart.

"So, to what new rock bottom do I owe the pleasure?"

"I know you're going to judge, and you should. But, as you know, I'm trying to print my dissertation. I'm most of the way done, but . . ."

"Okay."

"Well, the printer ran out of paper and it's beeping and beeping and the sound of the machine makes me wild. So, I just need a little more paper to finish, but you know I can't go to the Department of Supplies because I'm not supposed to be using work resources to print my dissertation, obviously. You know Marge in Supplies is a gossip, so she'll squawk to Old Spots. Then they'll examine my department's paper usage, and alarm bells will ring. Someone will come knocking: 'Just to check a few discrepancies,' Old Spots will promise. But he'll be there to stick his snout into the whole department and my existence in it. They'll use it as an excuse to get me gone. You know I can't lie for dung. I stutter all over myself and spill the truth. So then"—Mitchell listened to Alfonzo indulge in the worst-case-scenario game—"I'll be fired for abuse of city resources. I won't be able to make rent, and Mr. Buzz will evict me. I'll become a homeless doctor of urban studies. And no one will hire a paper thief to teach impressionable undergrads."

Mitchell scrunched his brows. At some point, you just have to jump in to interrupt your friend when he's caught in an angst groove. "Stop. You're making my headache worse. What can I do to help?"

"Blank sheets. For the printer. I swear I'll replace them. No one will ever know. This whole thing was a mistake. The machine is beeping, and my dissertation's due this afternoon. I need to get this done before it all migrates even further south."

Mitchell riffled through his drawers. "I've got it. How much you need? I've got about a hundred sheets—that good?"

Alfonzo lay his head on the cool desk. He groaned. "This is useless. I need about a thousand, or eleven hundred. Or, I mean, to be precise, I need twelve. Twelve hundred sheets." It felt as though he were admitting to a wood pulp addiction, or gambling debt.

"Buddy! Why the hell are you printing it here?"

Alfonzo was hopeless. "I know. You know I know it's a mess."

"I don't have that much. You just said it. They're sticklers in Supplies."

Alfonzo butted his forehead into the desk. "I'm sorry to put you in this position. I'll wait until the next deadline. It's not my season. I'll go unplug the machine." Alfonzo held his breath. They sat for a while. Mitchell's red plastic fan whirred on the desk.

"Okay, let's not get overdramatic." Mitchell tapped his toes. "I have a few questions. The deadline is today?"

Alfonzo snorted yes.

"You're going to give this to your thesis adviser?"

"Yes."

"Mr. Writing Pad?"

"Dr. Vinograd."

"Same same. What would happen to this copy? If your adviser accepted it?"

Alfonzo explained that if the document was accepted he would be asked to make more clean copies that would then be bound and submitted to the library. This copy was just a stepping stone.

"Is he easygoing? You like him?"

"Yes. I mean—why?"

Mitchell hummed. "What I'm thinking is that I give you this stack of scrap paper I've been saving for another purpose. It has some information on one side that's not important. If you can use that, I have enough. You can tell Lilypad the situation. Frame it as an environmental act. Then later you can give it back to me. When you don't need it anymore."

Alfonzo reflected. He would feel strange explaining this to Dr. Vinograd, but perhaps it would also be good camouflage. More words on the flip side of his words would make the whole document even more daunting. He wanted desperately to be done. After it was accepted, he could print the dissertation on fresh paper. He imagined Dr. Vinograd annoyed but ultimately accommodating.

"But why would you need it back?" Alfonzo asked.

"That's between me and my cod."

"You doing something fishy?"

Alfonzo calmed. They joked that he could spin it as conceptual.

"Tell the good doctor you're using recycled paper on purpose, as a comment on bureaucratic waste and the trampling of institutional memory under the hooves of a callow and destructive administration."

"He'll love that. I'll tell him it's like a smudgy, papery form of the psychoanalytic writing tablet. A palimpsest."

"I don't know, but sure."

"You're saving my life," Alfonzo hummed as Mitchell pushed a box of papers to him.

"I have a favour to ask in return."

Alfonzo worried this would get complicated all over again.

"I want you to change the title of your dissertation. You never took my old suggestions seriously. Call it 'Made in Llamerica.' It's gold. Or maybe, 'Coming to Llamerica.'" Mitchell chuckled. "Or 'The Bright Llama.' Get it?"

"Subtle. But it's schoolwork, not an album. I have to be serious."

"My friend Alfonzo is saying no jokes? What's the world coming to?"

"No jokes, for once."

By late afternoon, the ship was righted. Alfonzo had appeased his printer with Mitchell's imperfect sheets. The Aztek Howtek finished. Alfonzo autopiloted through the rest of the day's filing. At 4:03 he slipped out of the Hall carrying the stack of papers and caught the train to Hunter, arriving at the department secretary's desk at 4:49 p.m. The secretary bird clicked her tongue but accepted his submission.

"Congratulations, kid."

"Woot?" He couldn't believe he'd made it. His legs were matted with sweat.

"Get yourself a drink." She closed and locked the door behind him as he exited.

Alfonzo found himself dazed on Park Avenue. He hopped on a train to meet Mitchell at Bamboo Palace.

In celebration they overordered. The raccoon waitress kept bringing out dish after dish: lichen dumplings, corn noodles, mineral-fried broccoli, moo shu forbs, and shoots and leaves panda-style. The camelids chewed and chewed. Mitchell humoured Alfonzo as he waxed nostalgic about his relationship with Viviana. He didn't roll his eyes when Alfonzo said that they should have gotten married, that she was the perfect one for him. Mitchell didn't remind his friend that it was Alfonzo who'd broken up with Vivi. It wasn't the time.

The waitress brought a plate of orange slices and fortune cookies with the bill. It was the restaurant's way of telling them to get the hell out. Alfonzo loved the abrupt message of the sweet fruit.

At the bar he made it through one drink before

ducking out. Sometimes this business of survival was too exhausting for words.

ENCLOSURE

8.

September light entered Alfonzo's apartment in narrow bluish beams. They prodded him conscious. He passively resisted in his warm straw bed, but the beams kept at it. The sunlight was in cahoots with his father. He wouldn't put such an alliance past either of them.

Fine, fine, he hummed in resignation. Anyway, he could not be late. He struggled up from the straw and toward the French press.

His father lived out in Ozone Park, in the same house Alfonzo had been raised in. Every couple of weeks Luis would guilt Alfonzo into coming out for breakfast at Libertad Diner. They'd started this after Alfonzo's mother died. He felt too sad to resist. Alfonzo was, in his heart, a dutiful son, though he dreaded the ritual.

As he finished his coffee, Alfonzo wondered if it was jacket weather. The temperature had been see-sawing between seasons all week. He opted for no jacket because the day before had been muggy. He locked his door and stepped onto the stoop. Peering around instinctively for predators, he saw only his neighbour, a frowsy goat in a blue sweater, pushing her grocery cart full of carrots. The wind was a touch Canadian this morning. He shuffled back and forth. His coat was now behind a double-locked door. The die was cast. He couldn't afford the time it took to go back.

The trip to Ozone always took a while, even when the MTA was running seamlessly. And the Metropolitan Transit Authority obeyed no animal's wishes for ease. The system was all seams. It was caution-yellow strips warning animals not to jump or push. It was wood benches shellacked with generations of public secretion. It wasn't that the trains didn't work; it was that they didn't want questions about where they'd been and why they were so late. The trains wanted privacy. The trains considered themselves a natural phenomenon.

Sometimes one train slipped into a station across from another train like they were two silver fish of the same school. But just as often, one train would enter the station with just enough time to give its passengers a glimpse of its fellow disappearing into the depths of the tunnel. You could not assume coordination. Yet no matter the vagaries of the weekend subway, Alfonzo would hear static from his father should he arrive late.

A notification flapped at the station entry. Leaves and garbage swirled as Alfonzo tried to decode it. In multiple languages, the sign alerted passengers of track work, delays, and buses filling in for trains out sick. He slowly assembled the words into a plan. The R wasn't running, so he would take the K to Jay Street and then transfer to the A. *Okay, okay, okay*, he hummed.

He thought he understood as he descended into the underworld. But then no. A rat family dressed in matching blue as if on a team chattered in the corner of the platform. They, like him, looked into the tunnel expecting, no, yearning for the yellow lights of some train, any train to appear, but none did. The K was supposed to be running over the R line, but no K ever came. At the end of his patience, Alfonzo climbed the stairs and doubled back to the nearest F/G/H station, only to arrive there just as an F was pulling away. As he silently cursed the rolling disaster of infrastructure funding, an H arrived. He calculated and felt relieved. He would still make it. He transferred from the H to the P, then after a few stops to an A, and found a place to sit in the corner of the car. Only forty-five more minutes to Ozone Park. He crossed his toes.

The train ride lasted the length of two *New Yorker* features. The first detailed the workings of an international criminal group known as the Fancy Bears, who were thought to be responsible for the biggest maple syrup heist of all time. Despite the comic sound of their crime, multiple beaver and elk had been kidnapped and abused during the theft. The Fancy Bears did not sound like nice creatures.

The other article was about Ocean Melt Greenland (OMG), a government research initiative to study ice. According to the article, Earth's ice was melting at a much faster rate than previously predicted, and the animals aboard an OMG research ship were extremely worried. When they attempted to share their findings with the government, OMG funding was abruptly cancelled. Since their initial trip, two of the researchers had died, one by drowning and the other by choking on a twig. It was sinister, but the officials interviewed insisted it was all unfortunate coincidence.

Through his sleepiness, all Alfonzo could muster was a vague "we're so fucked" feeling. When the train got to the Ozone Park stop, Alfonzo shook his back and brightened his face in preparation. He wanted to keep things positive for his father's benefit.

Ozone was where both Alfonzo and Mitchell had grown up, and where all their relatives still resided. It was vestigial. A dewclaw neighbourhood. An inert leg hanging off the body of Queens. An indefinite somewhere with yards and parking spots where golden pollen swirled down from the many privately owned trees like yellow snow in a snow globe.

The neighbourhood was a speck of foam within the bubble of New York. In his dissertation, Alfonzo had written at length about a theory of urban bubbles. For a bubble to be, it must have interior, skin, and some atmosphere or substance called *the outside*. The form requires tension. The inner substance presses out, while the outside substance presses in, but they remain distinct because of the membrane. In and out yearn to touch and blend, but the skin prevents it, at least until all the tension proves too great.

Bubbles are economic and metaphoric; they are made with saliva or rubber, soap or blood. Bubbles multiply, merge, burst, and form afresh. Life would be impossible without this structure. Earth is a bubble of rock and water spinning within its own fluid, gaseous, clinging film of an atmosphere. Bodies are themselves bubbles made of different-sized bubble-like organs, cells, and other wiggly globules. Alfonzo had barely passed high school biology, so maybe a real scientist would protest his imagery, but he thought this theory poetically true. So what if technical terms refused to stay in his head? The universe was bubbles all the way down.

It was common knowledge that an invisible medium—like psychic oxygen—flowed through the city. It was an effervescent, intoxicating substance. In Manhattan, the centre, the air was so abundant it changed animals' behaviour. It made them buoyant and prone to hysteria. It gave them outsized confidence and naive optimism. The animals at the far edges, however, suffered from a lack of clean air. They moved slower and wheezed heavier. If Manhattan was a nested series of hollow spheres, then Alfonzo had grown up in one of the outer layers.

In the third grade, Alfonzo had learned that the word *ozone* meant something beyond his home. That day in class was the first time he'd collided a small reality with an environmental, even cosmic, thought. His teacher, Ms. Malanga, stood before the class and explained a big poster behind her. A green-blue ball with white clouds and brown continents. A red sticker where they were. Ms. Malanga pointed her nose there and said, "Home." Alfonzo and his classmates nodded. Above was a light blue layer punctuated with birds and raindrops. Another layer held a yellow balloon, then golden orbs representing meteors, then wavy purple-white smudges meant to be light. The outermost area of the chart was a deep blue-black dotted with white stars. Ms. Malanga pointed her nose at the orb layer and said, "Ozone." The class oohed. Ms. Malanga was an excitable auburn collie who favoured patterned bandanas. Alfonzo's dad called her a fellow traveller. She was his favourite teacher in grade school, and he remembered fondly all the animals in class drawing posters illustrating different aspects of the natural world. Ms. Malanga described the invisible gases cocooning the planet, each layer serving the purpose of protecting and facilitating life. The ozone was like a fine shield, she told them. It was a rare but significant gas, like a celebrity or a gifted soul. The planet needed all these bubbles, Ms. Malanga explained. Without them, life would be impossible.

One day Ms. Malanga told the class that there was a hole in the ozone and that everyone was making that hole bigger by using hairspray and air conditioners. She described the effects of refrigerants and solvents, Freon and foam-blowing agents. Alfonzo asked if it was like the hole in his sweater or the one in the middle of a frozen pond. But Ms. Malanga answered no, it was not like that. There is no actual hole, but more like a thinning patch, an area of wispy fragility, like a father going bald. One little goat named Raquel got so upset about this lesson that she started to cry. Her dad repaired air conditioners. He complained to the principal, who in turn reprimanded Ms. Malanga. Alfonzo's mom huffed that boneheads like Raquel's father would rather see the world end than change jobs.

After that, Alfonzo would perk up whenever he heard

TV reporters mention the ozone layer. It felt personal but also galactic. He imagined that his neighbourhood had some vital responsibility in protecting the planet. Alfonzo liked imagining the sky's layers. To soothe himself he pictured all of Earth's creatures tucked in safe under the atmosphere's wispy gaseous blankets.

Everyone learned about the existence of the ozone layer at the same time that they learned it was burning up. It was like learning someone had been alive all this time by reading their obituary. When Alfonzo became a teenage Red, he thought back critically to Ms. Malanga's emphasis on individual responsibility. He decided this kind of singular focus was bullshit that just drew attention away from the overwhelming-yet-hidden damage done by corporations. As a teenager, and still to this day, he blamed the corporate entities for just about everything.

Libertad Diner of Ozone Park, Queens, had silver siding like a submarine. A sign spelled out its name in blue neon. It was his father's default spot. He'd been a loyal customer for ages, but since Gina's passing, Libertad had become his de facto dining room. The interior was decorated in wheat-and-olive hues with flourishes of tomato red. The place resembled a Naugahyde sandwich wrapped in tinfoil.

Alfonzo's father, Luis, sat reading the *Times*. They both looked at the clock.

It wouldn't have mattered if Alfonzo had showed up on or before the dot; his dad would have already been there. He was forever before him. Luis arrived for trains and buses with hours to spare. He went to movie theatres early enough to watch the slideshow of local advertisements that played pre-trailers. He ordered drinks before happy hours began. He was always already there, reading the paper. Being early was no small matter to Luis. It was a key indicator of one's morality, professionalism, respect, and capacity to succeed. Luis assumed that those who were late were wastrels. He'd been born before his due date, and if he had any say he would have liked to die early. Alfonzo suspected that his father hadn't entirely forgiven his mother for getting to the afterlife ahead of him.

Luis did a shame thing with his eyebrows that caused Alfonzo to slump down into the booth.

"Have you heard from your cousin?" Luis asked.

"No, why?"

"They're expecting another baby."

"That's wonderful."

"You should have congratulated them."

"I'm hearing about it right this second."

His father hummed something like "That's no excuse."

"I reserve my time machine for important shit."

Father and son stared. Here was how his father prodded him.

Alfonzo hadn't loved any creature since Viviana, and Luis still considered their breakup a personal affront. Viviana was the should-have-could-have-been mother to Luis's non-existent grandbabies. Both of Alfonzo's parents had yearned for another generation to dote on. When his mother died, his father channelled grief into this issue of the failed coupling and the marriage that never was.

"All your mother wanted was to live long enough to see you happy and successful."

Alfonzo rolled his eyes. His mother, he said, wanted to stay alive for life, not to see her son repeat a story. His mother loved love, Luis would tell Vivi, ignoring his son.

Alfonzo wondered still if he'd rejected Vivi to hurt his father. After their breakup, Luis called his son a fool and wouldn't speak to him for months. When they got back to some kind of relating, Luis would drop in questions about new mates. At holidays, other family members would join in the chiding. "When are you going to marry and have young?" his aunts would ask. His cousins, Hernando and Alan, would also get in on the game, but with more subtlety. They'd chew their grass lumps while casting him a you-poor-sucker look. They'd point him in the direction of that llama waiting tables or the sheep paralegal who was so-and-so's sister. "She's sweet," they'd promise. Alfonzo reacted so poorly that eventually the family gave up.

Back when they were kids, his cousin Hernando had talked a big game about how he would live a life radically different from that of his parents. He had played bass in a goose punk band called Gaggle Reflex. He wanted them, he and Al, to travel to Patagonia, or at the very least to hike Mount Katahdin. Anything to get out of the dirty city grind. Who knows, his cousin fantasized, they might even fall in love with animals far outside their species. They'd seen Hernando's brother, Alan, dabble in that kind of behaviour in college by falling for a fox bartender. Both the fact that she worked as a bartender and that she was from the Canidae line had caused a minor family scandal. "I like her just fine," Alfonzo's aunt grumbled of her son's relationship, "but come on, she eats mice! Literally!"

As they'd aged, Alfonzo had watched Hernando succumb to the social pressures of the herd. Very little of his youthful yearning was evident in his current life. What was saddest to Alfonzo was that he couldn't even get Hernando to admit to the old dreams. He called his old music stupid. Alfonzo insisted it was psychedelic brilliance. Hernando was now a dentist in Floral Park. He mostly hung out with Alan, a forever square who worked as an account manager at Bobst Hospital. Hernando had a job his mom approved of. He had the thick wool belly of his father. He jogged but then stress-ate too many fried vegetables and followed them with too many grass beers. Alan was an avid catnip smoker. After his kids went to bed, he would sit in his basement and get high while watching nature documentaries. He called this his hobby. Alfonzo called it depression.

At family gatherings, Alfonzo would drink along while listening to his cousins try to convince him to join their way of life. It was time for him to get serious, they argued. He would feel better as soon as he strapped on bags of debt and started the long walk toward retirement, and beyond that, Alfonzo presumed, death.

Luis agreed with Hernando and Alan. They were what he could have been, if only. If Alfonzo had listened or heard, absorbed, or behaved. If Alfonzo hadn't been beguiled by liberal arts classes on chromatics and empires. If Alfonzo had known his place, he'd have one. If you came from a rich uptown family, it was all well and good to go searching for yourself in a foreign land or to make sound art with hummingbird collaborators, but these kinds of practices were off-limits to the working class. Wanting them just muddled the natural order. You go to college to get a job. Or, at least, this was what Alfonzo imagined his father thought.

Alfonzo would rather drown himself in the East River than end up like his cousins. Luis sensed this but never mentioned it. But *snob* hovered on his tongue like a seed never spit.

Alfonzo took solace in Mitchell. Mitchell walked the same path with lighter steps. Mitchell's mother yearned for grandchildren to treat more lovingly than she'd ever treated Mitchell. Mitchell's mother was the only one in her mah-jong circle without fluffy grandbaby photos. But Mitchell shrugged off the pressure.

Luis regarded his son over his newspaper. Alfonzo had his mother's tendency to brood. Luis loved his son but felt it was wrong to hum those particular feelings.

"Shall I order us some alfalfa?"

"Sure," Alfonzo hummed.

"I miss your mother," Luis said.

"Me too, Pop."

After breakfast and a goodbye head-butt, Alfonzo left his father to his Saturday afternoon of baseball on the radio. The train came right away, and Alfonzo folded himself into a corner seat. It wasn't as if he needed his father to remind him of his mother or Vivi. He thought of them plenty. His father could not let subtext go unspoken. The train rattled through its black tunnel.

Both his mother and Viviana had come from the mountain heights of South America, where alpacas truly belonged and Alfonzo had never been. He could not help but think of his mother as a storybook character. Her life had a folk-tale quality, and death made her even more mythological.

Eugenia "Gina" Abastoflor was born in a village where her ancestors had lived since the ancient camelids crossed over the land bridge, forever ago. Alfonzo himself would have been born there, too, if not for the troubles. His grandparents Selestino and Naira had never dreamed of leaving the mountain, had never wanted New York, when they welcomed their baby daughter one gleaming April morning.

The young family was innocent. Alfonzo could not imagine the story otherwise. They were far from the capital. Their village was a speck in the Technicolor expanse of the altiplano, and they were happy in it. But their joy was to be shattered. A civil war, fomented by American interests, was brewing. It had to do with oil, mineral resources, ideology, fruit growing, land control. Government-backed militias swarmed across the mountains. The llamas and alpacas of the village hummed together in fear. A neighbour's cousin planted the image of New York in his grandfather's head. In America they could be safe.

A band of guerrillas slaughtered animals in the next village. They didn't eat them but left the corpses lying in the fields or draped over fences. The government denied involvement. Selestino and Naira made their decision to leave. They did not want to die without meaning. They did not want their daughter to die, ever. They filled their packs, set out down the mountain, and headed north on foot.

Alfonzo ached when he pictured his mother as she would have been, a kid with skinny legs and honey-coloured wool, donning a little backpack and toddling off down the mountain behind her parents.

This odyssey took them across each America: South, Central, and North. His grandmother told stories of the humid streets of Panama City, where her bag of precious mementos was stolen by a spider monkey. Many times, his grandmother had wanted to stop. She loved the palms and cacti of Coatzacoalcos and warmth of the locals. She would have liked to settle there but could not convince Alfonzo's grandfather to let go of his northern vision.

All that way, his mother as a little alpaca walked along without complaint or tears. His grandmother, though, suffered. She was sick by the time they reached the town of Flower Mound. His grandfather gave almost all their money to get them a ride in the back of a hauling truck from Texas to New York, the destination his grandfather had decided on because of a neighbour's cousin.

New York, the cousin had said, was big and safe. And in a sense, it was that for Alfonzo's grandparents. They were able to disappear into the herd of Peruvian immigrants. They met a network of guinea pigs and llamas and tapirs who stuck together and who empathized with and protected the newly arrived. They found a place for themselves in the woolly underbelly. New York absorbed the Abastoflors into itself, and for that Alfonzo would always love the city.

They'd arrived when New York was in a period of crisis, but because they'd left a greater crisis, in which heaps of bodies were left to rot, they took the city's crumbling in stride. They sent Gina to school and pushed her to succeed. She was a model student. She was even valedictorian of her class at St. Dunwen High School for Girls. She went on to start a degree in animal psychology at Brooklyn College, but then she met Luis.

Alfonzo's dad had been handsome in his day, and he had a fast way of talking that charmed this serious immigrant alpaca. They got married pretty quick, and his mom left school. Alfonzo knew it was because his mother got pregnant with him.

Later, once Alfonzo was safely in grade school, his mother enrolled in a program at LaGuardia Community College to become a dental hygienist. Alfonzo could sense, without anyone ever coming out with it, that his grandparents were devastated their daughter hadn't finished her four-year degree.

Alfonzo going away to college awakened something long dormant in his mother. Out of the blue she enrolled in some continuing-ed classes, then decided that was insufficient and leapt into a full-degree program. She finished the same time Alfonzo did. Much to the family's surprise, she kept on. She enrolled in a master's program to become a therapist. All of a sudden, his mother wanted to share ideas about what she was reading. She told Alfonzo about the theory of learned helplessness, about Harlow's experiments, and the mirror stage. She grew her wool full and fluffy in a Peruvian style. She started wearing bold colours and silk scarves with flowers and fruits. Gina had an adorable mom-style. All his friends thought so.

A cancer diagnosis would have been shattering no matter what his mother had been doing. He would have mourned and raged no matter what. But somehow the illness felt more cruel because it attacked just as Gina was in the midst of self-transformation. She had been so happy and free.

The doctors explained lymphoma and its stages.

Alfonzo was never curious about the cancer. He had lived life as a model student, but when it came to this illness he turned dull. He refused to study it because no matter what he learned, the cancer would still kill her. He had felt sure of this. The doctors explained palliative care. Alfonzo plucked strands of grass from his wool and arranged them in a pile on the desk.

Luis, in contrast, became Gina's self-appointed specialist and spoke of disseminated lymphoma, carcinomas, and total nodal irradiation over dinner to his silent wife and son. He made Gina stop wearing her signature perfume, and he threw out the throw rugs lest the dust hurt her immune system. He cut foods from her diet and added foods: corn was out; beets were in. He saved a folder of articles about antioxidants and free radicals and the benefits of green tea. He prepared chopped salads with lemon. Gina pushed her plate away and cried. She didn't have an appetite; everything tasted like sand. She only wanted ice cream, green-tea flavour if possible.

For a while the disease was invisible, until she began losing wool. She became skinny except for her stomach, which swelled and hurt. The skin above her knees sagged, and she bruised easily. Her cancer was ever-changing; in phone calls, Luis spoke in numbers. Alfonzo just hummed along. *Numbers up* was bad; thus *down* was good. Not like the stock market, like a debt. But whom did Gina owe? She seemed to be making payments with her hair and her fat, with her saliva and her ability to stay awake.

Alfonzo accompanied her to the grocery store, where she studied packages.

"Your father wants me to buy ancient grains and says I can't have potatoes anymore."

"Get what you want, Mom."

Alfonzo's head ached all the time. Gina bought only a carton of banana ice cream, because the store had no green tea.

"Don't tell your father," she said.

Who was in control? No one.

Alfonzo went with his parents to doctors' visits. The doctors talked in war metaphors. Her territory was occupied by internal enemies. Her immune system didn't know how to battle the insurgency. The cancer changed form and disappeared into the civilian population. The doctors sent in pharmacological reinforcements. Gina had to fortify herself, they said. The doctors recommended further treatments that would, they said, trick her body into fighting harder.

Instead of reading his father's clippings or the doctor's pamphlets, Alfonzo read a scholarly book on metaphor. He read that war wasn't an appropriate trope for illness, yet it was the most popular.

He thought, though, that maybe it *was* right, just not in the way generally thought; that maybe there was something to be salvaged from the military image. There were plenty of parallels—just not ones to which the doctors alluded. Cancer was like war in that both were brutal and nonsensical. There was no such thing as a just cancer. Innocent beings who happened to live next to power plants got tumours they didn't deserve, while chemical executives got to live in gated communities and drink clean water and avoid cancer's reach. War and cancer both involved metals and carcinogens, poisons and blood, coloured ribbons, charities, and lawsuits. They both had treatment centres and therapy groups for survivors and family members of survivors. Many professions existed supposedly to end war and cancer but also to serve and support those who were affected. Governments and hospitals and businesses profited from the growth and development of both war and cancer even as they proposed ways to eradicate them.

The system wants to kill us slowly as it wrings our bodies of every last drop of value, Alfonzo hummed to himself. *My mother is just another one of their wool rags.*

His dad did everything by the letter. His mom was the most positive fighter the hospital could ever ask for. But she still died. At the end, when she was not in great pain, it was because she was stoned out of her gourd, and when she was not stoned out of her gourd, she was in great pain. Those were the options they had.

The night Alfonzo's mother died, he and Vivi were at a concert.

All these little details were etched in his mind. The serious audience of birds and sheep and cats dressed as if they worked in a factory that produced utopian toys, with abstract squiggles and leaflike shapes dotting their jump-suits and kerchiefs. That had been the style of the season.

The singer they'd assembled to see was a thin dog with a thick, wavy black coat. Before she sang she told the audience a story and explained how it had formed her conception of music.

The singer talked about remembering and forgetting as a form of composition. She remembered hearing an old country song from puppyhood. She forgot the words. She made sounds like what she remembered. It was an invented memory, a translation of time. Her youth and her adulthood. The singer described the evocative power of contrary-motion string bending. She stuttered, and Alfonzo remembered being touched by that vulnerability.

Her voice wavered as she spoke of the quality called natural sustain.

The dog then recounted the time when she first heard the Montevideo Symphony play *Amériques*. It had come to her on a portable radio at the beach. This experience, like hearing the country song, had changed her life's direction. Moments such as these were why she was onstage. After this lightning-strike moment of listening, she bought the score to the great orchestral piece and vowed she would figure out a way to sing it by herself. An impossible task. We have to start somewhere impossible, she said.

"My music comes down to the question 'Can I be multiple?'"

And then she began to sing.

After the concert, Alfonzo and Vivi had strolled back to their apartment, stopping a few times to nuzzle necks. They were drunk and happy. The sidewalks were still wet from rain that had fallen during the show. It was the beautiful turning of summer into fall.

Outside their apartment Alfonzo smoked a last cigarette. When they entered their dark living room, the phone began ringing. It was his father, and Alfonzo could hear the tears.

"Where are you?" Alfonzo asked.

"Maimonides Hospital." His father's voice was laboured and husky with phlegm. From just the inflection and blockage, Alfonzo knew.

When Alfonzo and Vivi had entered the experimental-music venue, his mother had been alive—sick, but alive.

Alfonzo had known her death would come; he'd been bracing for impact. But all the clenching was useless. It was impossible to stay always on guard.

His and Vivi's apartment was quiet and dark; neither of them flipped on the light in their haste to get the ringing phone. Vivi stood frozen and watchful. There it was, the night his mother died. The blow wasn't a hard one, as he'd expected. Grief came over him like an enveloping mist. It wrapped around his neck and entered his lungs. He found himself drenched with sweat and sobbing.

His mother had just collapsed and died in his childhood home, and when it happened he was unaware at a concert. Alfonzo would never forgive himself for this. Vivi entreated him to be kind to himself. But he could not.

When Alfonzo got back from Ozone Park, he called Mitchell to say he needed to get wildly drunk that night.

"Did you just have a Luis breakfast?" Mitchell knew the score.

Alfonzo groaned.

"You're in luck, my friend, because it happens to be the birthday of our dear colleague Dawn Delamarche."

"I was hoping for more of an anonymous hole-in-the-wall-based bender."

"You're coming."

"Well, where is this celebration?"

"The Ruby Fang."

"Dear dog, that's the opposite of what I want."

"Ten, you anti-social fleabag."

"No need to name-call."

"See you."

9.

The Ruby Fang was located atop the Pastoral Building, a hotel on the far West Side. The name came from the shape—the building was a pointy curve, with the top few floors made of red-tinted glass. The architects had intensified the general effect by lighting the tip from below. At a distance the building really did resemble the tooth of an animal. But it was a lonely fang surrounded by squared-off, more herbivorous shapes. The gum line of the neighbourhood was crowded with boutiques, restaurants, and nice apartments. This neighbourhood used to be the docks. Zone of rutting for money, import and export, smuggling and blood. These streets had been sanitized, and now a mural of donkey labourers was the only thing that referred to this neighbourhood's old flavour.

While Mitchell popped into a bodega for cigarettes, Alfonzo waited outside, studying a luxury advertisement that read "We live in a golden age of pants."

Alfonzo's grandparents had avoided coming here for fear of hearing rude propositions, or getting mugged or trampled in some spontaneous stampede. Alfonzo now avoided the area because it made him feel poor and angry. Proximity to the moneyed filled Alfonzo with dread. He didn't have to fear direct violence, as he did in other neighbourhoods. Rather, he reacted to all the menace that lay hidden. While chatting with rich animals, it was too easy to forget that what they had was derived from exploitation of workers, or plastics, or oil, or the manipulation of addictions, markets, or politicians. Abuse ran underneath wealth like utility wires and pipes beneath city streets. Alfonzo wasn't worried about getting robbed; he was afraid of being infected by the bad logic of those fancy animals.

"Is Dawn, *you know*, or is she just aspirational?"

"Well, she's from Westchester, so you draw your conclusions," Mitchell drawled. "But this is only a party. Relax. Maybe this will be a chance to meet someone cuddly."

Mitchell was trying to help, but when it came to affection, Alfonzo could only think of Vivi. Viviana Lopez-Cuña, poised daughter of leftist vicuñas. Like his mother's family, they were émigrés who ended up in New York. But unlike Alfonzo's upbringing, Vivi had grown up among artists and intellectuals. Vivi's father became something of a celebrity in America. Vivi's parents had settled upstate in the town of Bovina, but they retained a worldly glamour that transcended the rural surroundings. The Lopez-Cuña household was rustic and formal; ancestral rugs hung on the walls beside fine drawings made of insect blood and berry-juice ink on bark paper. Vivi's father had a library and smoked a pipe. Alfonzo was intimidated and awed by the family. No one else had yet mesmerized him the way Vivi did.

He'd loved her for her beautiful confidence, her sense of honour. Vivi had loved him, he supposed, because he was a scuzzy punk from the city and she collected weirdos. But later they found they shared an essential desire for justice. They both liked to poke at authority. With her, Alfonzo felt protected. She believed in him as a thinker. After college, they'd rented an apartment in Gowanus and joined the food co-op. Vivi got a job at a non-profit teaching poetry at public schools. They decorated from thrift shops and their parents' odds and ends. They hosted their friends for Malbec and grass. They pantomimed grown-up life. There was an image in their heads of how adult animals behaved. But then, as they sank deeper into it, Alfonzo felt the pressure intensify. Why not go to Argentina or do volunteer work in the Himalayas? she asked. How would we even get there? Alfonzo shouted. She said, By boat. But how would we even pay for it? It wasn't really a fight about transportation.

Little things accumulated. They fought about security and direction. She demanded answers Alfonzo didn't have. Alfonzo felt he had to find a stable job and stick with it. She was disappointed and he was exasperated.

He had to stay in the city; that's what adults did. After his mother died, he collapsed inward. He'd stay out till all hours with Mitchell. With Vivi, he couldn't string a conversation together. She accused him of cowardice. She reminded him they were still young and could still go out into the world. He said he wasn't rich like her, so he didn't have the privilege of swanning around like a spoiled brat. The breakup was a slow drift. Vivi went to visit her parents, and Alfonzo said maybe it was best if she didn't come back.

Even though it was his doing, Alfonzo still wasn't over it. Death and separation, the two illuminated each other. Mothers and lovers in the eyes of young males. Oppositions and symmetries. He had been an idiot.

Mitchell cleared his throat; he didn't want to listen to Alfonzo hum on and on about Vivi like he always did. She was a sweet vicuña, but it was a lost cause.

"Buddy, I want you to join me in the present. It's all right to let go."

Alfonzo apologized for being stupid. They skirted a heap of garbage by stepping into the road, only to hear shouts from a pair of weasels hanging off a carting truck. A cloud of music puffed from a poodle-themed bar.

"The least you could do is try to be friendly. Maybe you'll meet someone sweet." Mitchell believed in making friends.

"I don't want sweet; I want revolutionaries."

"Sure thing, Carlos the Jackal."

They entered the dark hall at the base of the Pastoral and went through to an elevator that stood like a portal to some underworld, though in this case Hades was located above. The over-under world within the tip of a tooth. That's how it was in cities. Little doors led to vast complexes. Bubbles swelled up inside larger bubbles.

Alfonzo shifted, antsy, while Mitchell conferred with a bouncer, a grim-lipped Doberman wearing a chain around his powerful neck. Mitchell assured the dog that Dawn Delamarche had put their names on a guest list, but the dog insisted on double-checking. Mitchell would have gotten in regardless, as he had a dash of fashion, but Alfonzo would definitely have been barred without Mitchell. He was too schlubby young-middle-age bureaucrat with post-punk leanings. He gave off that metaphysical dirtbag stink. Under the appraisal of the guard, he realized he also gave off an actual damp-straw smell. He should really get some fresh hay for his apartment.

The dog finally gave them a reluctant go-ahead. They squeezed into the elevator alongside a couple of Persian cats, a greyhound in a three-piece, and a delicate pony with an up-do. They all inhaled and stayed silent.

The elevator shot upward. The doors opened into a massive circular room, with windows all around and glimmering aquariums bisecting the space into smaller zones. Everything—the aromatic candles, the shelves of liquor, the groomed fashion animals—communicated discreet excess. Despite—or perhaps because of—the line of animals waiting on the street to get in, the bar was not crowded.

Mitchell disappeared in search of Dawn. Alfonzo wandered toward an aquarium. It was taller than he was and stretched half the length of the room. Multicoloured gravel covered the bottom. A dark blue fish hovered in a yellow light. The fish was round like a miniature planet; orbiting him in the water were smaller moonfish and the dust of a thousand food flakes. *He is depressed*, Alfonzo decided, then chided himself for projecting. Could one read a fish's face? What did he know about fish feelings? But then, did one need to read an expression to imagine that being trapped in a glass box for one's entire life would be a horror? It didn't take a mystical empath to imagine the fish was miserable. It was obvious.

Through the narrow tank he studied the blurry forms of other bar-goers busy in pantomimes of leisure. A circle of dogs sniffed one another's ears and asses. On a carved fake branch two eagles groomed themselves, pausing after every few strokes of beak through feather to stare at each other. Beside a potted palm stood a motionless horse. The plant seemed to be its own kind of captive creature, one whose body was a single leg topped by a head of green frond hair. Just another transplant. Alfonzo caught himself in a mirror as the dark blue fish in the aquarium jerked down through the water and into a fake rock crevice.

In the last few years, animal society had exploded with furious debates about the ethics of aquariums, and of the question of sea-life sentience in general. What *are* sea creatures? Are they animals like us, or are they different? What do we owe them, if anything? This unsettled conflict between land and sea had a history that stretched back to ancient times, but it had been newly stirred up by Hurricane Sparky. The arguments were furious and had far-reaching implications. There were many factions. Alfonzo tried to follow the subject by reading the *Atlantic* and *Barker's*, but sometimes he found it too depressing.

Some animals became entrenched in the position that aquariums were harmless, even kind institutions. These animals contended—in letters to the editor and in quasi-academic treatises—that they were motivated by the pure and altruistic desire to keep fish and other "lower beings" safe. They on the land should act as caretakers for those aquatic animals who were capable only of drifting through existence. This position had powerful backers, including the city's own Mayor Shergar. He was known to be a great aquarium lover. So much so that he had installed luxury aquariums in his many residences and in his office in City Hall. When he was first campaigning, Shergar chose to stand beside a tank with a few small sharks for his first magazine photo spread.

Then there were others who made no claims to altruism. Scientists who devoted themselves to testing whether sea creatures could even feel pain. Philosophers who argued that even aquatic mammals weren't deserving of respect, being turncoats who'd abandoned the true struggle on land. The sea was a maternal embrace, and so they were eternal infants: only those on land had grown up.

Foremost among these thinkers was the gibbon Martin Kürbis, who wrote in his famous *Soil and Paw, Water and Fin* that we must judge animals by what lasting things they create. Sea creatures didn't have farming, mining, or industry of any kind. The seas didn't have writing, tools, or cities. "We cannot blame fish for this lack," he wrote, "because they are by nature simple." Any ire he had was reserved for aquatic mammals: traitors to progress possessed of the brainpower to contribute to bettering life on Earth but content to waste their potential flippering around in the water. Seals, dolphins, and whales, he claimed, were traitors to the mammal cause. Their ancestors had walked on land, developed lungs and higher brain functions, and then crawled back into the womby wetness when the going got tough. They'd chosen to spend their time mingling with the boneless and the spiny, the water-breathing and utterly alien creatures of the deep, and with that they'd consigned themselves to the role of the dominated. It was therefore morally acceptable for land creatures to keep them, and indeed all lower creatures, in tanks. After all, the sea was just a meaningless churn of life and death, so what difference did it make?

There were those who resisted anti-sea arguments, but the opposition was fractured. There were the reptiles, already marginalized on land, who pointed out that they had many biological similarities to sea creatures and yet participated in land society. There were a few sea mammals who came up to speak about the unseen riches of the depths. There was a movement of small vegetarian creatures, rabbits and mice and the like, who argued that size should never be an ethical determination of consciousness, but they often found themselves shouted down by coevals who were only too happy to let the carnivores eat from the sea so long as it minimized such violence on land. Others went further and argued that making distinctions between *any* creatures was the beginning of a slippery slope that would always lead to cruelty, intentional or otherwise.

According to the government, the sea could not be recognized as a state actor because its denizens never responded to the various invitations to debates, treaty proposals, and conferences the land creatures had extended to them. They wouldn't engage meaningfully in a political process.

Alfonzo and Mitchell had both heard the sea-life conspiracy theories. According to some, like Lenny Old Spots, the sea was a breeding ground for death cults, for violent and poisonous and gelatinous anti-land-animal conspiracies. Believers argued that aquariums allowed sea creatures windows onto the land. The puppet masters in the sea were using these tiny sea creatures as their eyes and ears. According to lore, they were watching and waiting for their moment to strike against the landed species.

Regardless of one's opinion, the aquarium arguments were politically heated, so for this place to be filled with fish tanks was a bold *fuck you*. They could just as well have had a banner reading FISH CAN GO TO HELL.

Alfonzo steered clear of aquarium arguments, but anyway, they didn't usually come up. Aquariums were for others. Animals who ate fish had to sort out their ethics, whereas he could remain neutral without much effort. It was an argument for the rich and the fish-eating to have.

Alfonzo tried to avoid looking because it made him feel guilty, but the glimmering water drew his attention again. The tank was mesmerizing. Besides the fish, it was home to translucent, slippery sea plants, artificial yellow coral, and a few grey creatures with antennae he supposed to be shrimp. There were also a few unidentifiable hot-pink and blue undulating somethings, pulsating star-shaped globs. Whether they were flora or fauna, Alfonzo couldn't tell. They looked poisonous and vulnerable, gelatinous and melancholic. Tendrils of semi-transparent plants hailed him from behind rock formations.

Alfonzo chewed a bit of Sichuan grass he'd saved from dinner. His anxiety had dissipated. Standing within this fang overlooking the city, Alfonzo sent his thoughts uptown to his dissertation sitting in his adviser's office. He had completed a great labour and now he was at a fancy party. It was sometimes nice to look down at things from within the head of the beast. He felt proud of his feat of willpower.

Mitchell sidled up.

"I'm glad you dragged me here. At least it's an experience."

"Fantastic." Mitchell beamed. He was always ready to be happy. "And let me finagle drinks. I'll find a way to get us economically faded."

Over the next few hours Alfonzo consumed many of Dawn's special birthday Moscow mules. He allowed himself to be buffeted by the gusts of other guests. A raccoon from the Office of the Actuary regaled him with details of inter-office political games on the second floor of City Hall. He concluded his monologue by asking Alfonzo if he liked peach schnapps, then ordering two cocktail shots called water moccasins. Alfonzo didn't know if he liked peach schnapps, but he accepted and drank what he was given. He wondered if this animal, whose name he hadn't retained, had real friends, and if so did he treat them in this domineering fashion. The raccoon let out a hoot after they drank, then announced his departure by grumbling something about pizza. As his new friend trundled off, Alfonzo realized he'd misplaced Mitchell. He commenced a wander-around.

Dawn the birthday deer leaned against the bar, whispering with a cat. Alfonzo had seen the orange tabby around City Hall and knew he worked in some communications capacity. He had that lustre that lent itself to smarming around with journalists. Dawn beckoned Alfonzo. She was all giddy.

"I am honoured that the elusive alpaca has deigned to appear."

"It's not my fault they don't let me out of the basement."

"You having a good time?"

"Delightful. Though I think I'm on my way out."

"Stay!" Dawn commanded.

"I'm wobbly on my pins," Alfonzo demurred.

"Hair of the dog," Dawn's cat friend chimed.

"I think that only applies the day after. Not in the midst."

"Miles and I were just talking philosophy. You're interested in that, aren't you?"

The cat insisted on buying a round. Dawn used the opportunity to introduce Alfonzo to Miles Tigger from the Office of Media Relations, and Alfonzo realized he should have snaked away without goodbyes. Now he was on the hook for at least one more mule or moccasin. One couldn't refuse, or at least Alfonzo couldn't.

"Miles and I were just discussing the Good Boy method. I'm but an aspirant. He's been at it a long time."

"Guilty as charged."

From what Alfonzo could glean through the deer and cat's animated joint recap was that the Good Boy method was a self-improvement organization centred on the teachings of a single dog. He had been a champion Westminster athlete who'd nearly destroyed his life bingeing on peanut butter and chocolate. In a moment of clarity, he'd quit everything and decided to get to the bottom of what it meant to be "a good boy." He'd gone on a quest across the country to "smell the shit," as Miles put it, of various religions and practices. He talked with snakes who sold oil, bald eagles purporting to possess perfect vision, and wolves who advocated going back to the woods. After the dog's journey, he returned to the city and founded the FOG-BOW Centre—for the Foundation for Good Boy-Oriented Work—housing it in a building off Union Square decorated with tapestries, potted plants, and an indoor fountain.

What this seeking dog taught at his centre was that animal nature was cruel, selfish, and wild. That modern society kept everyone in a constant cycle of panic and indulgence. Murder and decadence lurked beneath every exchange. Only through intense self-discipline could an animal gain mature awareness and overcome this cycle. Only by making oneself one's own Good Boy could one rise above the suffering herds.

"So what does 'one' do at FOGBOW?" Alfonzo inquired.

With wide eyes and in enthusiastic tones, Dawn and Miles described a regimen of primal barking, coordination and focus exercises, and long-distance group runs. To strengthen one's inner Good Boy, Alfonzo learned, one should set goals, remember names, and sniff others deeply. One should develop emotional will (EW) by asking many questions. One shouldn't waste time with frivolities. And if one followed the advice and became strong of body and mind, then one was a Good Boy destined for wealth, both spiritual and financial. Many of the powerful animals of New York were known to visit the FOGBOW Centre. Movie stars, business creatures, and politicians scampered in and out of the place.

Dawn promised adopting the philosophy would change Alfonzo's life. Good Boys invariably sniffed out success. The method had shown her how to be her own parent. "When your inner puppy whimpers, you will be empowered to say, 'Yes. You *are* a Good Boy!'"

Though Alfonzo scoffed, this mention of parents troubled him. His mother would have said he was a good boy regardless, and it would have puffed him up. But he could admit this, he thought.

"Does all the canine talk bother you?" Alfonzo warbled.

"It's not meant literally," Dawn said. "*Dog* doesn't mean 'dog.' *Dog* means 'all.'"

The cat chimed in: "The principles are grounded in dog reality, yes, but other animals can still use the framework. We're the same underneath, aren't we?"

"We all want love," Dawn yelped.

"And happiness," Miles added. "We gather together as Good Boys to foster positivity and encourage self-mastery."

"Yes!" Dawn enthused.

"But it's not a free gathering." Alfonzo felt himself getting hot with annoyance. "Isn't it expensive to practise being a Good Boy with you all?"

Miles licked a paw and swiped it behind his ear. "I would turn that around and ask, how much is goodness worth to you?"

"So not *all*, then?" Alfonzo poked.

"The money is just symbolic," Dawn insisted. "All who want to be good can be, if they make it a priority. Really, the world is divided into the good and the soon-to-be good. Once you start investing in yourself, it starts paying dividends quickly enough."

Alfonzo gazed around the mostly empty bar. In the shadows he spied Mitchell beside an aquarium. The tall black llama was studying a floating red gelatinous creature. Behind the bar, neon pink and green squiggled. Soft air blew from a hidden vent. Alfonzo imagined himself walking away from this mounting conflict, taking the elevator to the ground floor and hailing a cab to ferry him home. He wanted to be cradled. He wanted to be transported by the magic of a professional driver to the safety of his straw bed.

From beyond the aquarium, through the glass and over the river, New Jersey flickered. These faraway and nearer blobs of light shimmered as indicators of residence, infrastructure, and commerce. They came together and were pressed flat by the wall-sized pane. He and Mitchell caught each other's eye. Mitchell winked.

Alfonzo didn't want a fight, or at least that's what he told himself, but because of school, or grief that always turned into vexation, an argument was an easy garment to slip into. What did it mean to be good in this rotten society?

"What about fish?" Alfonzo asked.

The cat, smirking, settled down on his paws so that they disappeared beneath his warm orange chest. "Anyone can join if they open themselves to the process. The Good Boys have nothing against the water beings, provided they come in with an open heart. You've got to ask, is it really us who have shut them out? Or have they closed themselves off from us?"

Despite his projection of confidence, Miles's hair was bristled up. He was clearly restraining some violent impulse with regard to the alpaca. "See, Al, under the method, you would come to see that your sarcasm is just your inner bad dog barking. It's maladaptive."

"Fish could already be Good Boys, Alfonzo! *You* don't know!" Dawn pressed her chin against her long brown-and-white neck. Tears had sprung into her big Bambi eyes.

"Look how you treat your friends," Miles meowed.

Dawn raised herself upright. She was taller and longer than Alfonzo, with fine reddish hair and a sculptural body. Alfonzo felt squat and dark and knock-kneed under her gaze. He felt ashamed, but also a little impressed by how badly he'd mucked up this situation. She tossed her head and glared at him.

"To find yourself is a struggle, Alfonzo. Before the method, I had a pack of inner wolves chasing me every moment, trying to drive me ever deeper into the woods of self-hatred. You want to twist it against the sea, but I don't accept your premise. Good Boys aren't like that.

"I was born a part of a herd, but I also had to find my joy pack. Maybe you want to wallow in the olden days and only see others' faults and weaknesses. But I want to spring into the future. The method works. I've seen the shiny coat of success. I've seen all kinds of beings gleam, okay? Not because they're rich or famous, but because they've learned.

"Happiness is about learning to catch whatever life throws at you."

Alfonzo spent the day after Dawn's party curled fetal in his musky hay, wondering if he'd ever been so crucially hungover.

HORSE AND SPARROWS

10.

Memories of his mother cluttered Alfonzo's dissertation. Each was small—a bauble, a treasure, a joke—but together they formed an overwhelming inheritance. Alfonzo had too many but couldn't let go. He studied each in the shifting light.

When he was young, Gina had told him bedtime stories. They would sit together in his tiny room while Luis watched baseball or public TV documentaries in the living room downstairs.

Alfonzo's mother liked folk stories best. There was one about the moon and the sun, who were married yet distant. Another story was about the adventures of King Jaguar. And yet another was a comedy about a family of musical guinea pigs and one foolish toad. In Alfonzo's favourite stories, camelids were heroes and heroines. It was a llama, according to his mom, who saved all the creatures during the Great Flood. His mother filled his imagination with animals who looked like them and possessed unique tools and quick wit. As he drifted off, his young self conjured mental images of a brown alpaca with curly wool springing along steep, lush mountain paths with a sack full of magical blue gems.

In one of Gina's stories, the Milky Way of the Southern Hemisphere was a world filled with animal figures. There was astral toad, serpent, fox, mother llama, and baby llama. One of mother llama's cosmic tasks was to drink up water from the ocean, then redistribute it to the mountains as rain. Sky llama had to drink and pee to keep the world in balance. But then one day the baby llama wandered away and got lost. In her grief, mother llama drank up the whole ocean and then began to cry. She could not stop.

Down on Earth were two alpaca brothers who spent their nights observing the skies. When it began to rain, they recognized that this cosmic mother's grief would wash away life on Earth if they didn't act. So they raced to the animal villages, sounding the alarm; they ran into the jungle and out to the plains; they circled the lakes and traced the rivers. They gathered up all the animals and led them into the heights. All the while, the tearwaters rose.

Up on the mountaintop huddled all the condors and tapirs, the dogs and pumas, the tamarins and bears, the mountain cats and tinamous and guans, the woolly monkeys and guinea pigs, the dusky-headed parakeets and golden-headed manakins, the butterflies and moths, the ants and spiders, the sloths and night monkeys and chinchillas, the bamboo rats and the elegant rice rats, and the cloud forest grass mice, the lesser bulldog bats and greater bulldog bats, the caterpillars and red and grey brockets, the jaguarundis and the delicate slender opossums, the turtles and beetles, and everyone else. They put aside their ancient squabbles for a time and talked of survival as they watched the waters rise ever higher.

Up in the sky, the baby and the mother found each other after much searching, and only then did the mother's tear rain cease. When at last the sun emerged and the waters receded back to the oceans, the creatures returned to their ruined homes, strengthened by their friendships. They built new societies across the drying lands. But even as many years passed, the creatures did not forget the brave acts of the alpaca brothers who had saved animal-kind.

Gina told her son that one message of the story was that it was the alpacas' duty to guide others through this world awash in grief.

Alfonzo realized after his mother died that all her stories came from a book of mythology of the Andes. He'd always thought she had brought them with her in her memory from childhood. He realized the Andes were in many ways as much a dream to her as they were to him.

These stories continued to pull. He analyzed them. He wrote glosses for his dissertation.

He was in his childhood bedroom under the green comforter. In this dream, he had fleas. He had mange. An itch on his knees caused him to thrash and cry out.

He was in his apartment. Someone was outside pushing every buzzer, one after another. From the second floor, his neighbour honked, "Shut up." The front door to his building slammed, and Alfonzo woke to Monday.

Too early to rise, too impossible to return to deep sleep. He tried to doze, but the neighbourhood would have none of it.

The ceiling squeaked in time to his upstairs neighbour's jumping jacks. The goat kids from 3A were taking turns doing flips off the basement's metal trapdoor. There was no point yelling, as it was their before-school ritual. He listened to their mother clatter downstairs and scold them off. He could hear her bleats grow softer as the family disappeared down the block. After that drama resolved, the mechanics across the street began revving the scooters they were mechanic-ing. Then the wind blew over a trash can. The fall weather had been schizoid. Yesterday had been cold, but today it was likely to break ninety degrees Fahrenheit. The morning radio said there was a hurricane watch.

Alfonzo crawled from his straw to make coffee and prepare. He'd taken the morning off from work in order to go meet his esteemed adviser, Dr. Oswald Vinograd. They had an appointment to talk about the dissertation.

At the Hunter campus security desk, a scrum of animals pressed impatiently for clearance. The main guard was a hawk who took the job too seriously. Beside him was a goat named Bluebell with whom Alfonzo had become friendly over all his comings and goings. He switched to her line to check his ID. The hawk glowered from his official perch.

"You look like garbage," Bluebell observed. She meant it in a sweet way.

"It's my day of reckoning."

"Okay, good luck, baby. But do yourself a favour and comb that wool before your meeting. Look in the mirror, for dog's sake!"

"Everyone hassles me about my hair."

"Aunty impulse," Bluebell said, and shrugged.

Alfonzo took the elevator to his floor, a quiet one that was home to Urban Studies as well as Audiology and Hydrology. The carpeted halls were their usual eerie empty and led to closed, nondescript doors. The only signs of life were the cartoons, quotes, and flyers that hung outside the offices. He skimmed advertisements for semesters at sea, an announcement of an upcoming colloquium on accelerationism, and a *New Yorker* cartoon featuring two dachshunds and a balloon dog. Punctuating this maze of halls were sad lounges. Every school Alfonzo had ever been to was furnished with the same pumpkin-coloured chairs that squatted around these leisure areas. There must have been some conglomerate called Fur-Nature Co. doing gangbuster business a few decades ago. Their shape and solidity belonged to a lost era of manufacturing confidence. Like the Aztek Howtek printer back in City Hall, the chairs evoked nostalgia for a time when animals believed institutions and the modern objects that filled them would endure forever.

The various white doors in the lounge led to identical shabby offices, each shared by many adjuncts. Alfonzo could hear them nervously scratching away at stacks of student papers. From these inner adjunct rooms, there was no way to tell if it was sunny or raining out in the world. A view of street life was not a perk available to underlings. Natural light was reserved for department heads. Views belonged to bigwigs.

Dr. Vinograd's office was in a farther hall, one that faced the street. Alfonzo shifted his feet on the dense grey carpet. Fear had made him early. Though the professor's door looked the same as all the others, it was in actuality the portal to the den of one of the university's most famous scholars. Vinograd received the old-fashioned support of the institution—time off to write and to give keynote addresses in distant cities, a bevy of grad students to do his menial tasks.

Swirls of fluorescent light energy swam when Alfonzo lolled his head back. The nausea from earlier returned in his gut. He scrambled to the bathroom, praying no one was there, and glanced beneath the stall doors for paws or hooves before quietly vomiting up a tightly packed grass ball. It made him feel better.

He dipped his face into the faucet, shook off, and straightened his tie.

He had waited and worked for this moment. It was time.

"Calm. Deep breaths," he told the alpaca in the mirror.

———

The office door was open when Alfonzo returned. Hazy light haloed the large dog dressed in rumpled professor drag. He beat his tail against the door frame as he waited to greet his most problematic advisee.

Dr. Vinograd's office was a burrow of scholarship. Every time Alfonzo visited, the number of books and files had grown and the empty space had shrunk proportionally. Mounds of paper sat fading beneath the window. Tree-sized stacks of books swayed as the door closed. A careless paw or hoof could upset the whole ecosystem.

The forest was made of books sent for free by academic presses and acolytes of the professor. Vinograd's own collection squeezed together in the nooks and shelves. Alfonzo could not understand how Dr. Vinograd found time to read about Procyonidae abstraction, fruit imagery in pre-colonial art, the theory of non-silence, and post-Kokoian linguistics, in addition to keeping up on his research interests. This was a professor always busy applying for—and winning—grants and awards. He had just been named the Hackler Foundation chair of the department and was going to teach abroad for a semester at the Wolf Liberty Hum Centre.

Once upon a time, Alfonzo had been allowed to borrow some of these books. This special privilege was reserved for students in Dr. Vinograd's good graces. Alfonzo had some time ago stumbled out of such graces.

He saw *A History of the Black Rat Market*. Alfonzo had pored over that text two summers back. On another shelf *Nose Logic and Cryptic Noise* leaned against *The Crisis of Globalized Monkey Business*. Of course, Vinograd had

Hooves of Iron, Hooves of Empire, and *Honeyed Tongues: Bees in Literature and Life* on display. When borrowing, Alfonzo had always taken special care never to read the professor's books around coffee or food. Just the sight of these familiar works grounded him. Maybe someday they could exchange books as colleagues, maybe even as friends.

"Let me just . . ." Dr. Vinograd ducked under his desk.

There was a burst of energetic rustling. Alfonzo wondered if he should be helping somehow. A disembodied tail wagged like a periscope while the hidden body continued to sniff out something. The professor growled, then popped back into his seat holding a paper bag.

"Dried grubs?"

Alfonzo declined.

"They're organic and wild-collected? Maybe these guys died of old age. But that doesn't make sense, does it. Isn't a grub a baby? Anyway—you should try one."

Alfonzo explained he'd already had breakfast.

"My wife insists I eat healthier. She's trying to turn me insectivorous."

The dog began crunching away.

The professor's black fur was grey around the temples and jowls; a fine thread of spittle hung from one curl. Alfonzo marvelled at this creature who had so much power over him and generations of students and yet so often appeared loose and sloppy. He was lovable, but Alfonzo had always sensed he was capable of biting his throat. Vinograd excelled at staring without blinking, and Alfonzo shrank into himself as the professor studied him.

According to biographical texts, Dr. Oswald "Ossey" Vinograd was a mix of black Russian terrier on his mother's side and Turkish herding mutt on his father's. They'd both immigrated to New York, raised their son in the Bronx. He'd gotten into Columbia and formed a chapter of the Young Animalists. He was an outspoken and charismatic activist. The end of his college years corresponded with the riots and strikes and protests that preceded Napoleon Herbert's political fall. Vinograd had occupied administrative offices and sung resistance songs to protest pig domination. He had been arrested but quickly released. He went on to get a PhD, also from Columbia, in French animal consciousness. He married a fellow student, an Irish setter from the public health department; they had two puppies.

He got a tenure-track job right out of school. But though he had spent his whole life within the public and private education system of New York, he never let go of the self-image of outsider, a rebel. He wrote about unlearning and unteaching. He barked out lectures on the need for play and non-hierarchical structures within the academy. He received tenure at Hunter. He bought a classic six apartment when the market was depressed. He wrote a book called *Sacred Saliva: A History of Dog Violence and Healing in the New World*. It caught on in the popular culture, and he became a fixture in a certain lecture circuit. He railed against austerity. He got a divorce and rented out his uptown property, then bought a little place in the East Village. Those were his bachelor days. He became chair of the department and sat on committees. He got remarried. His new wife was one of his grad students—he hadn't meant to fall in love like that, but his colleagues were very understanding. His two children from his first marriage finished private school and moved on to Dartmouth and Skidmore. He invited members of the Grandjouan horse separatist movement to give a famous series of talks. He went on sabbatical to Tarragona and smoked catnip with Mineau Ritta. He and his new wife had a litter of three puppies and he made jokes about being an old dad. When the department suffered cuts, he rallied the faculty and bemoaned the decline of public discourse. He hired adjuncts and tried to lift their spirits—he knew what they were up against. He suffered through his son's foray into rock and roll, then pills, then recovery. He wrote yet another book. He and his ex-wife helped their son buy a fixer-upper in a scruffy part of Brooklyn, saying the manual labour would do him good. He had dinners with the dean and the president of the university. He took on new grad students. He began to relax more after so many years of hard work.

"What do you think of your dissertation?" the professor asked his student.

"It isn't perfect. But I created a chain of connections, questions, and propositions about a group of animals and their place in the city. That felt important. I thought it important to finish up. As you've said, a dissertation is a step."

"Toward what?"

"Completion?" Alfonzo stuttered.

Vinograd consulted a notepad. Alfonzo's dissertation heap sat on the desk. Troublingly, there were no coloured Post-it notes poking out.

"The university has recently implemented the C-R-A-D method of analyzing student work. Is your work C, concrete? Is it R, reasonable? Is it A, affirmed by scholarship in the field? And finally, is it a D, a deliverable our department can stand behind? Now, I know how CRAD might sound."

Alfonzo hesitated.

"I mean, between you and me, CRAD is wretched. But I had no say. This comes from on high. Committees agreed. But if we put aside the name, it does give us something useful to work from. Just ignore the acronym and hold on to the underlying intentions."

"CRAD." Alfonzo nodded. "I didn't know I was supposed to be reasonable."

"We're all supposed to be reasonable now." The professor nosed another grub from his bag, swallowing the thing in one go. "Alfonzo, I want to spare you the waiting. Your dissertation is not CRAD. I have decided not to advance your dissertation to the committee . . . You've written fifty pages about clouds as the breath of a sky llama."

"Only to unpack it as an ancient metaphor for the condensation cycle."

"It would be better if you just listened for now."

"Sorry."

"You asserted that money was shit."

Alfonzo wanted to clarify that what he'd written was that seabird guano was once upon a time a highly valued commodity that fed the Peruvian economy. In certain instances, bags of shit were used to buy goods. He was just being descriptive when he said a great deal of shit circulated in the economy. But it was in the text. Dr. Vinograd knew how to read. Alfonzo did not interrupt.

"You write of grief and mothers and fathers without articulating why this belongs in an urban study. And your chapter on bees who feed on tears and how that is like memory was deeply perplexing. And what do padded toes have to do with the body without organs? What does childhood have to do with the Chicago school? You are asking the reader to connect the dots between silence, second-hand time, Heifers International, and scapegoats, basement shows, and debt. And then!" Vinograd sighed as he flipped through some pages. "And then, midway through, you blend what appear to be financial charts into your text. But you never explain what these numbers mean. They just sit there on the adjacent pages, forcing the reader to puzzle through. What does the cat bond market have to do with alpaca affect? What does Seahorse Company $13.8 million or Dusty Leaf Holdings $75.65 million have to do with your mother's cancer? You juxtapose all this as if we'll understand, but it's just mystifying."

"I should have clarified about those numbers." Alfonzo struggled to remember the explanation he and Mitchell had joked about. "The double-sided nature of the text was supposed to mimic ancient palimpsests. I was reusing pages from the bureaucratic machine, and in so doing playfully making myself into a kind of bricoleur. I was denaturalizing the reading experience?" It was coming out wrong, and Dr. Vinograd was smacking his tail under the desk in irritation.

"I'll be honest, Alfonzo. I feel betrayed. I thought we talked about what you were to do as my student. I thought we had an understanding. Specialize, I advised, and instead you scattered. Be cautious and deliberate, I said, and instead you made wild and unsupportable emotional assertions. You have written"—the dog searched the air for precise words—"an abstruse tangle of embarrassing length, when I told you to write a concise and sound study. There are little flashes that are wonderful, but overall this project is maddening." Then, perhaps realizing how harsh he was being, Dr. Vinograd drew back. "Like you, your dissertation is fascinating but chaotic. For many semesters I have defended you in committee meetings, but I cannot protect you any longer. How could I ever put this forward as CRAD?"

"This is a fluid time? My generation knows only the regurgitated version of ancient stories, and the new stories don't yet make sense. I tried, I truly did. I wanted to make you happy, but how could I make sense under our present conditions?"

"It was your job," the dog replied.

"I was overwhelmed by the interconnectedness of all things," Alfonzo mumbled.

"In a different educational climate, a different era, you might have been able to find a suitable corner in academia.

But now the kind of scholar you wish to be no longer exists. This is a tragedy for all of us. Now there is a pressure I didn't experience when I was starting out. You have a latent resistance that has bubbled up in a way you perhaps cannot even see yet. My analysis is that you are sticking to your youthful vision, but your current self is in conflict and trying to break free. I don't want this to cause you despair. I think this is an opportunity for you to put your mind to work in the real world. Take a good look at yourself, Al."

Dr. Vinograd began telling his favourite anecdote about a snake that had been shedding its skin but then became trapped. Alfonzo had heard it before. The reptile had circled for hours in a tunnel of his old skin until a neighbour found him and called an ambulance. In this telling, Alfonzo was the snake, twisting and twisting inside a circle of himself. His ordeal, like the snake's, had become a joke, but he was living within this spiral and was tired.

"Is this about the ending?" Alfonzo interrupted.

"Think of this as a life's new beginning!" Dr. Vinograd responded, only to launch back into a story about a time his wife got caught in an arm of her own sweater.

When Alfonzo had last cried, it was about his mother, and he had been alone. Whenever the urge to cry struck him in public, he would work out the feeling in another way, buy another drink, jostle someone on the train, spit into a rain grate. But now, before he had the chance to bury his impulse, tears had burst from his eyes. They streamed down his fur.

"It pains me as much as you to be in this position, but the text is too long. It strays across disciplines. If I were to pass it on, the committee would tear its stomach open and eat its entrails," Dr. Vinograd said. "I am close to retiring. I want to guard you, to guide you back onto the path, but to be frank, I no longer have the energy. I appreciate your mind, Alfonzo, but I wonder if there was not a part of you that wished to fail. You have lost the thread, and I worry that if I let you—enable you to— keep going, you will become more and more lost in the wilderness of your own thoughts."

Alfonzo hoped his wool would absorb, that his body would conceal the body's reaction, but Dr. Vinograd saw the tears. It was all over.

The dog came around the desk to comfort Alfonzo. He gestured at the tissue box. "I know this is upsetting."

Internally, the alpaca shrieked at himself, *Stop this leaking, you weakling, you infant, you pathetic worm!*

"Thank you," Alfonzo said with a sniff.

"You'll do something great. Just not in the university."

Alfonzo struggled to his feet abruptly. A column of books trembled as he shoved his rejected work into a bag. "I should be getting back."

"You don't have to hurry off," Dr. Vinograd entreated. "We had to get through the hard part, but I would like to help. I would like so much to give some life advice."

Alfonzo would sooner have thrown himself off a cliff

133

than listen to anything more. All he wanted to do was make like a tree and leave.

"I have to get back to the office. But thank you again for everything," Alfonzo said, hoisting his rejected tome. The 1,532 pages of it strained his tote.

"I hope you continue to think of me as a friend," Dr. Vinograd offered. "My door is always open."

Alfonzo ordered his body out of the office. From down the hall he heard a door shutting on soft voices. The climate control system burbled. He moved toward the elevators as if underwater. *Act natural*, he chanted to himself. *Put one foot before another. Breathe in. Breathe out.*

11.

Alfonzo wandered downtown in a daze. He let the currents of animal life carry him like a bit of flotsam. Flower shop, smoked-fish deli, hat shop, café, pocket park, bodega, bank, bodega. Business cat, delivery dog, deer who lunches, cow with a cart, pigeon, pigeon in a hat, rat. The city at eleven thirty on a weekday was indifferent to one alpaca's private catastrophe. But it was an open-hearted indifference.

His father had a great-uncle who, after getting fired, jumped off the Queensboro Bridge. Alfonzo was not going to do something grandiosely sad like that. No suicide. He had an urge to call Viviana. But ex-girlfriends don't want to hear from long-lost ex-boyfriends because their dissertations were rejected.

As he walked, the street atmosphere shifted between construction and commerce. Wholesale shops piled high with Statue of Liberty–themed knick-knacks, gold-tone belt buckles, scarves, gloves, and plaid slippers. A furniture store called Sleeping Dogs was going out of business. La Petite Beet was full of rabbits eating salads. Alfonzo passed a store of rhinestones, beads, and feathers called Strange Notions. Its window had a diorama of a Broadway stage with buttons and wires twisted into poodles in bikinis. The miniature dogs were arranged before a sea made of satin ribbon, with paper dolphins frolicking between blue ruffles. Alfonzo wondered about selling. One had to hustle many rhinestones to pay rent on a street-level retail space. Maybe the bead shop was a front for some other sort of more black-market-type business.

His paternal grandmother had been among the waves of sheep, rabbits, goats, and other alpacas who had once flocked to this neighbourhood to sell the wool off their backs. Their bodies fed the omnivorous clattering looms of the garment industry. His grandfather used to work as the night guard at a place on the corner of Twenty-Sixth. The building had housed small wool-spinning businesses and wholesalers for seashells. It had recently been turned into a hotel. Smokers hovered around office-building entryways.

He continued downtown. It was one of the farmers' market days in Union Square. There were the usual crowds loading their string bags with mushrooms and chard and apple cider. The park trees rustled their dry leaves over Hairy Krishnas who shook little bells as they sang.

Alfonzo turned. He didn't want to follow Broadway any farther. He paused at a news kiosk to buy water. The day's headlines lay in front of the style magazines.

PLASTIC: TOO GOOD TO TOSS?

MAYOR DISBANDS AFFORDABLE HOUSING
PLANNING GROUP

He zagged left into the East Village. A group of raccoons and goats ambled along chatting, and he slowed behind them at a polite distance. They were dressed in anarchist black. New School or Cooper Union, Alfonzo guessed. One looked familiar. Alfonzo might have seen him around Gowanus, or maybe at some lefty protest.

The creatures were engaged in an animated conversation.

"So," one of the raccoons said, "this little Shih Tzu, right—an absolute louse—comes up to us out of the blue and points to Muffin and asks, 'What is she even, an otter freak? A seal or something?'"

The goats dropped their mouths open at the raccoon's story.

"He asked what?"

"Yes, and then his weasel friend chimed in and was like, 'Maybe a dog knocked up a seal. I didn't know their kind were allowed around here.' And then he growled, get this, 'I'd like to see her wet.'"

They all took a long pause to register the horror.

"They were acting like we couldn't hear them," the raccoon continued, gesticulating with his paws. "Meanwhile, Muffin is mortified."

"Disgusting."

"I wanted to tear his nose open."

"Why didn't you?"

"I am an avowed pacifist. Even with tick-faces."

They all laughed.

"So, what did you do?"

"I tapped him on the side and was like, 'You forget that we all came from the sea. Your ignorance will not confine the rest of us.'"

"Baby, you were too nice."

"So enlightened."

"I would have shredded him."

"We cannot sink to their level."

"True."

Alfonzo studied the young activists. They had that mix of admirable bravery and arrogant conviction. Though their fur was greasy and they wore scuzzy art gear—one wore an Anti-Cimex band T-shirt, and another had a Battle of Mice patch on her bag—they had control and poise. Their jewellry looked heavy and well crafted. It took some amount of stability to commit to looking so artfully dishevelled.

How derelict had his own youth been? How many East Village squat shows had he braved as a dumb kid? He recalled a particular Gorilla Biscuits show and shuddered. He'd survived an adolescence in the bad New York, only to see it become a harmless shell with hardcore trappings. In his adulthood, he'd devoted so much time to decoding what this city had been and was becoming. How many books on subcultures had Alfonzo read? How many had he skimmed? And how many books hadn't he read but pretended to have so that he could impress some other dodo grad student at a party? He knew more about what these activist kids were signifying than they did. He should be teaching. But instead—instead of having a place in the conversation—he was a bureaucrat in a cardigan. He was a pusher of papers, due back in the basement. He was a random with an unheard mind. He was an expert. Of what, he was no longer sure. He had feet in different realms. He did nothing well. His career had faltered because of school; his writing had slowed because of work. A half intellectual, half worker was an underwhelming chimera. His father was right, he was a snob. Alfonzo disappointed more than he illuminated. He didn't breathe fire; he just coughed up cigarette butts.

His dissertation was a secret he was telling the future about the present, but no one was listening.

"Did you hear about the Battery Tunnel?"

"Yeah, I knew some rattos down there. I think Templeton was living there."

"That's wild."

"Did they lose all their stuff in the flood?"

"I think so. There's a fundraiser concert."

"You going?"

Alfonzo had been staring without realizing, analyzing without thinking.

"Can I help you?" the raccoon barked.

Alfonzo jumped. They were talking to him.

"Pardon?"

"It's rude to gawk."

He apologized. "My mind was elsewhere."

"Well, it might be a good time to get present."

"Right. You're right." He shook his head and bounced across the street to avoid conflict.

The group filed into a café, casting critical glances over their shoulders as they went.

Alfonzo needed to talk to Mitchell.

12.

Mitchell was hunched over his desk nursing a maté and scowling at a photograph of his avowed enemy the honourable mayor, Baldwin Shergar III. Mitchell knew quite a lot about Shergar. He'd read memos from him, studied critical and rapturous coverage about his project to remake the city. The mayor was a political celebrity and essentially Mitchell's boss, yet Mitchell had never spoken directly to him. The llama often glimpsed the mayor's comings and goings in the Hall, a spectre flanked by security dogs. He knew the mayor but felt sure he was a nobody to the horse. This was how the llama wanted it. Know your enemy and be invisible. Mitchell recalled Sun Shih Tzu. "O divine art of subtlety and secrecy! Through you we learn to be invisible, through you inaudible, and hence we can hold the enemy's fate in our paws," Mitchell hummed.

Before him on the desk was the horse's long face in a flattering magazine photo spread. The llama hated this horse with all his being, not for who the mayor was—all right, that too—but for what he was doing to the city. Mitchell began to read.

THE MAYOR GETS DOWN TO BUSINESS

By Honey Pongo

It doesn't matter if he's just come from a marathon meeting with charter school leaders or from a ribbon-cutting ceremony at a wastewater treatment centre: Baldwin Shergar III is one of those horses who appears always freshly groomed. In any encounter with the mayor, you're confronted with a tall, glossy stallion in a uniform of pinstripes and silk tie. His greetings are forceful and clipped. This is a horse on a mission.

"Sure, if the mission is trampling over us," Mitchell grumbled. Shergar wanted to be mayor so he could tell the inhabitants of the largest city in the country to stand up straight, pay their debts, and hustle like their lives depended on it. He wanted to be mayor so he could strip away the social contract and implement a Horse and Sparrows financial structure: feed everything good to the few, and convince everyone else that sifting through whatever plopped out at the tail end could sustain them. What did this lead to but a few obese creatures and a lot of shit? Mitchell snorted again and kept reading.

As is well-documented, Shergar is one of the richest animals in the world. This is a fact he both wears on his finely tailored sleeve and downplays in conversation. He's not afraid to laugh loud or swear when he's feeling passionate. He has a common touch.

He was born into a prominent family, but in order to push their son onto his own path, Shergar's parents left their son only a minuscule inheritance. This mix of pri-vileged upbringing and financial restraint uniquely pre-pared our mayor for the dualities of running New York, a city of great wealth and poverty.

This was already insane. The paper was glossing over hard numbers in favor of polite obfuscation. Wasn't a small slice of an obscene fortune still a lot? Mitchell was no financial wiz, but last he checked $20 million was a pretty substantial amount to inherit out of college, or re-ally anytime. Mitchell chewed a grass ball furiously. He enjoyed working himself up.

Though it wasn't covered in the article, Mitchell knew that Baldwin Shergar came from a prominent line of rac-ing, military, and political horses. His great-great-great-grandfather on his mother's side was Thaddeus Blazer, one of the world's richest animals in his era. The robber baron Blazer had made his fortune with his company U.S. Horsepower, which dealt in alfalfa and steel. The ancestor Shergar trampled any animal, be they politician, rival, or undernourished labourer, who dared get in his way. He was for a time the long face of gilded exploita-tion. In his later years, though, he had become obsessed with legacy. He bought a newspaper and made his writers pepper it with tales of his charitable deeds. He paid for libraries and public watering holes for the great unwashed. For pleasure, he amassed a trove of looted treasures from South America and then donated it to the Met. His name was carved on the walls of this and other major city institutions.

Mitchell continued skimming. No mention of Mayor Shergar's ancestors. Perhaps the journalist considered it common knowledge.

What the article did outline in admiring detail was Mayor Shergar's first career in hedge funds, the realm in which he'd built his "minuscule" inheritance into his own obscene bundle of cash. It was only after jumping from Bear Capital to Leopard Ventures to MidOcean Partners, and tripling or quadrupling his net worth, that Shergar had turned his attention to politics.

All that mercenary work was glossed over. Mitchell searched for the story under the story. A rich horse wanted to run the city like a business. As if that were a virtue. What did that mean? Wage suppression? Layoffs? Hostile takeovers? Offshore accounts? Squeezing those who owe you while putting off those you owe? What values were to be gleaned from business? Mitchell wondered. But also—one didn't want to get distracted—a city is not a business. This isn't democracy.

> While Shergar has distanced himself from the boards and charities he once actively participated in, his wife, Brooke Saint Mars, has become more active. Some say she is the soft-power side in their partnership. The wife has taken to giving generously to shelters, food banks, and after-school programs.

While at the same time the husband is cutting funding to those programs, Mitchell raged. Mitchell despised the mayor. The newspapers raced after him, a pack of hounds with press passes ready to paint him as charming and visionary. Who cares? It didn't matter to Mitchell that the mayor was a real horse who itched at his withers and ached in his hooves. These destroyers of worlds were always in the end just sagging animals. That didn't stop them from being soulless. Those in power were just the distracting performers who covered for nameless conglomerates and banks and armies. It was so hard to name, to wrap his mind around, that he ended up humming it. A private song about language untethered from meaning.

The mayor spoke of deregulation. Mitchell translated that into heavy-metal-poisoned water supplies. The mayor spoke of public–private partnership, which Mitchell understood as selling off essential public services to the mayor's friends.

Honey Pongo, the reporter, asked the mayor about the issue of dark money. Shergar dismissed this as a problem with a nostril flare and a tail flick.

"I am not a politician by nature. Until coming to City Hall, I never held office or worked in government. So, I'm not interested in the smoky backrooms or the whole buildup of political favours—'You scratch my flank, I'll scratch yours.' If anyone thinks they can buy me, they're in for a rude awakening." The mayor insists his only interest is in good ideas, and if someone—be they lobbyist or average animal—wants to come to him with a good idea, he'll give them his attention. "If animals are putting resources behind an idea, it's because they believe in it, and I think it's my job to listen without prejudging the source."

Aha! Mitchell took a gulp of lukewarm maté. Here was a hidden principle, a shaping shard of ideology masquerading as common sense. There is no alternative. There is no separation between wealth and thought. We're all little buyers and sellers. You'll get the ear of the mayor if you have a good idea. There is no hierarchy. Did the mayor really believe this? Or was it just another cynical sound bite? Mitchell didn't know which possibility was worse.

To keep sane, Mitchell held close the concept of karma, a cycle bigger than everyday life, a slow cosmic rhythm of justice. One could not, he reasoned, get out unscathed. Maybe it would take centuries of birth and death, but sometime, somehow, the mayor's spirit would come to know what it feels like to be crushed by money. Mitchell needed to at least have a fantasy of justice. All this ambient suffering must surely come back to haunt the powerful who caused it. A mayor who signs documents that cost animals their shelter, that consign young creatures to violent shelters—that mayor should feel pain in proportion to the pain he causes.

Mitchell tried to believe in a slow but churning movement toward justice. But lately he'd been having a hard time with this. He'd become impatient. That day, like many days recently, Mitchell found himself wishing for instant karma.

The universe couldn't let this behaviour go. Could it?

Mitchell pictured the mayor's elegant office, only a few floors above his own. He pictured a bolt of lightning, a tree falling, the roof caving in, crushing the mayor at his desk. Mitchell wanted Shergar to go down in history as the mayor who tripped over a garbage can and broke his neck. He hoped that a swarm of wasps would slip through an open window and sting the mayor to death. He wanted the horse mayor to shriek and quiver like the simple animal he was. Mitchell wanted some wild cosmic event to bring the horse to a painful and freakish end. Mitchell wanted him to be reduced in his death throes to his basic animal senses, to know in that last instance that none of the money or influence he had accumulated could shield him from physical fragility. He wanted the horse to know it had all been futile and that if he was remembered, it would be only for his pettiness and greed. Mitchell wanted every sting from his fantasy wasps to awaken the mayor to the suffering his wealth had brought others.

Mitchell knew that death wouldn't end the philosophy of which the mayor was just a symptom. He knew others would emerge to take up the cause the instant the mayor fell. But still, Mitchell wished for it. It just felt wrong that evil assholes all lived to be tottering elders. It wasn't just that the good died young, it was that the bad lived forever. Few got what they deserved in this life. Think of Hissinger.

He closed the magazine and tossed it in the recycling, then opened a folder of applications for a housing complex in the Rockaways that had three vacancies and a wait-list fifteen hundred names long. He was supposed to go out there and inspect the place for a bunch of maintenance violations. He looked at the list: tenant intimidation and harassment, unlawful evictions, unlit corridors, extensive mould, repair work done at unauthorized times of day, broken locks. He took a deep breath and noted that the developer just happened to be the mayor's wife's cousin. *A total coincidence, I'm sure*, Mitchell hummed to himself.

From down the hall came a clicking trot. Mitchell waited for the knock that preceded a familiar head popping around the door.

13.

Mitchell was all wound up about the mayor, and Alfonzo didn't feel up to revealing what had happened with Dr. Vinograd just yet, so as they headed out of City Hall to get lunch, Alfonzo listened to his friend's familiar kvetching.

"Shergar is a swayback nightmare, sure, but the real problem is all the other schmucks who prop him up, who convince animals to vote for him. It's an abusive-father, big-leader situation. They think that by siding with the bully, they'll be exempt from his hooves. It's like some delusion that by trotting along behind, you, too, can one day be a boss. We'll be a world of bosses. Ha!"

"Umm-hum."

"And you know what's really insane is that article doesn't even touch sea politics. Post-hurricane policy is the real story, but it's just glossed over. Like 'Of course we're all united against sea aggression.' So, my question is, is there even such a thing as sea aggression? Since when did we all decide sea creatures aren't fellow animals? They tell this story as if it's always been the case, but land and sea have always been connected. It's insane. Have we forgotten there would be no life without the sea? 'Tough on the ocean' becomes the cornerstone of the mayor's appeal, and the journalist pretends it isn't even happening."

"*Hum.*"

"You know who probably ate up that whole article? Old Spots, obviously. I mean, I wouldn't even be surprised if he was that unnamed source praising the mayor. The pig would eat the mayor's shit all day and then scramble for breath mints if the mayor so much as wrinkled a nostril. *So sorry for my stink, Mayor,* that pig would say. Ugh, just thinking about Old Spots gets me all spitty. It's always the bullies who are also grovelling kiss-asses. You know what I mean?"

"*Umm-hum.*"

"He's such an herb. You know he comes to me every day to talk about water rights? Like would it kill him to recognize another creature's existence? I mean, it probably would."

"*Hum.*"

"I'm getting wound up. I'm sorry. I'll calm down. But actually, one more thing. It's that pig who's got the mayor's ear. That galloping hunk of ass-dandruff doesn't know anything himself, but he's surrounded by toady manipulators. I feel like we're losing it. In his memos, Shergar basically suggests we're all going to be drowned by aquatic sleeper cells. We have to take a stand. I cannot take much more."

"*Umm-hum.*"

Alfonzo and Mitchell manoeuvred around a family of French bulldogs wrapped in couture scarves. Beside them, a chicken stood nervously, peering uptown, waiting for traffic to clear. When the two friends finally made it to their favourite food cart, they had to wait in a long line to order and then in another to retrieve their orders. All the while, the urban menagerie streamed by.

"You're awfully quiet. Am I boring you with political commentary?"

"No. It's just, I went to see Professor Vinograd."

Mitchell did a little bounce on his toes. "I forgot it was today! I should be treating you to a fancy lunch."

This reaction made Alfonzo warm. He had a lifelong supporter in Mitchell. It made it worse, though, because he had not just his own disappointment and shame to digest but also the experience of seeing the news hit Mitchell. The sun filtered through the fur overhanging Alfonzo's eyes, making a little visor. He tried staring into the distance, but the distance was blocked by the colourful display in a Poochi store window. They finally got their falafels.

"Vinograd rejected my work."

Mitchell scrunched up his brow. "Okay, sure. But seriously, must I now refer to you as doctor all the time, or just when we're in public?"

"I'm not going to be a doctor."

"That is insane. Stop lying. Can you get a second opinion?"

"Getting a PhD isn't a terminal illness."

"Says you."

They chewed on in silence. Alfonzo hadn't asked about options. Why hadn't he asked? Dr. Vinograd's words felt final. It wasn't only the professor who spoke, but the whole of academia. It wasn't the academy's fault, though. His failures were his fault. Self-sabotage. Stupidity. An essential misunderstanding. Maybe Dr. Vinograd was right. He didn't even recognize his own instincts. He didn't even know if he was a ruminant. An unknown shadow alpaca lurked within the self he thought he knew. Self-saboteur. An aphorism flitted through his head: *There is another world and it is inside this one.*

"Who's in charge? You're going to find old Wino-dad's boss and you'll protest. You're going to resubmit, or re-edit, or whatever it takes. And if they ignore you, we're going to call a reporter and tell them the story of a city university giving up on a hard-working student just because he doesn't fit in with their cookie-cutter mode. You're no alpaca-scholar cookie."

Alfonzo hummed what he could not say. "I am not good enough for the university. I could not fit in. Every part of the academy whispered that I wasn't right. The fluorescent lights looked down on me. The papers cut me. The carpet tripped me. The library hid its serious journals. When the printer rebelled, I should have taken it as a sign. I am a meanderer, a grazer, and what they want are straight-line walkers, those with a strong sense of direction. I have been asleep to my true self."

"Okay," Mitchell nudged, "I hear you, though you're wrong. If you don't want to fight, then I won't insist. But you did seasons of writing dedicated to understanding animal life in the city. We need these stories. We need historians and thinkers to listen and guide us. I reject their rejection."

For the second time that day, Alfonzo started crying. He laughed and coughed to cover it up, but Mitchell saw.

"Here's what we're going to do. You're going to play hooky for the rest of the day, and you're going to come with me to do a site visit in the Rockaways. We'll pretend you're my assistant or something. We'll work this out. We'll have a time at the dangerous exciting beach."

Alfonzo considered. No one would come down to the Department of Records that day. No one ever came.

"Hum," Alfonzo agreed.

They stopped in at the Early Cenozoic so that Mitchell could whisper playful conspiracies with barista-lemur Pamella. Dawn came into the café and interrupted with cheek nuzzles; she had let the awkwardness of their fight about Good Dogs dissolve, and Alfonzo was grateful. Mitchell slid Pamella an envelope and an affectionate look, then swept Alfonzo out the door. The sadness of the day sensitized him to the joy of the outside, the smell of leaves and pretzels, other creatures' shampoos and their deeper hidden funks.

"Was that a love note?" Alfonzo teased.

"Of a kind," said Mitchell.

This excursion made Alfonzo buoyant. Subways could sometimes become something more than utilitarian tubes for transporting animals from home to work. Sometimes they felt like a magical escape pod. You enter your capsule in one neighbourhood world and emerge in an altogether different zone. Chelsea could give way to the Cloisters. The cramp of Hell's Kitchen could open into Prospect Park. The trains shot everyone through the ground. It was fantastical, really. There was so much of everything and it was all so strange. Alfonzo celebrated the muchness.

Leaving the centre revived him. Manhattan and the Rockaways might as well be different countries. One realm was devoted to business, the other to all things aquatic. The shadows of City Hall and Hunter College were not long enough to fall over that far shore.

Salt wind flapped the blue cloth of the Atlantic. It mussed their wool. Sun-faded tarps rippled and snapped around half-destroyed buildings. Sand skittered along, obscuring the lines of the road. Animals were pushed and pulled along by the wind. Seagulls joked above them.

Alfonzo and Mitchell looked up and down Beach 90. Mitchell explained that in one direction was the Atlantic Beach Bridge, and in the other was Beach 227, tucked behind the Breezy Point gates.

The usual city structures were faded and cracked. They—those animals in charge of numbers and names— seemed to have given up out here. The labels were functional: Beach Channel Drive faced the channel, while Shore Front Parkway faced the open ocean. The beach felt loose.

Out here, water was the true religion, government, and culture. But even though, or perhaps because, this was a stronghold of seashore life, marks of hostility were visible. They sauntered by a cinder-block wall with a mural of whales and octopuses and dolphins painted in blue, green, and purple. Someone had graffitied over it BUBBLE BLOWERS OUT NOW! Over that, another painter had written a succinct FU. Gull boom-bap blared from a car stereo.

Alfonzo hadn't been to the beach in ages, since before Hurricane Sparky. During that storm, he'd hidden out in Mitchell's third-floor apartment, where they listened to records and ate macaroni. They worried and joked about the Gowanus flooding into their building. It would turn them into toxic avengers, said Mitchell. Alfonzo responded that it would probably just give them cancer. They blew cigarette smoke out the window as rain battered the leaves off the trees. The Gowanus did overflow into some basements but never got as far as their building. Alfonzo returned to his ground-floor den and dreamed of black mould.

Out here, of course, the storm had been devastating. He'd seen images in the news. They'd become iconic. Dogs paddling for their lives, clinging to bits of wood and using upturned buckets as boats. A pod of dead dolphins lying among a broken boat. On these streets there had been fireballs glowing from broken gas lines. Wooden houses turned mushy as waterlogged phone books. Though the city had long since cleared the most dramatic wreckage, signs of the disaster remained. The most visible evidence of the storm appeared in absences: concrete foundations in weedy lots and ghost lines on walls marking how high the water got. Those stains and vacancies told a story of dark, neck-high water churned with ragged wood, seaweed, oil-coated garbage, and downed electrical lines whipping like industrial-sized eels. The water had been everywhere. It could return if it wanted.

Mitchell led Alfonzo to a bedraggled apartment tower and buzzed the intercom. Alfonzo realized he was fuzzy on what site visits entailed. Were there forms? Would they have to go into a crawl space? Did he have to wear a hard hat? Must they meet a super? Would someone yell?

Mitchell snorted. "Don't worry."

Alfonzo let go. The elevators were broken, so they took the stairs. He liked springing up behind Mitchell. Mitchell joked about mountains to climb. Just like Machu Picchu. His friend had a way of making everything feel like a comical jaunt.

When they arrived at apartment 1975, the door was cracked. Mitchell called out in his business voice. A faint meow came from within.

The creature was speaking, but whether it was directed at them or someone else was unclear. Mitchell tried again.

"M'ello? Can we come in?" Mitchell gingerly poked his head inside.

A response came louder than before. "We're back here."

The apartment was shabby, but it also had that charm of the old: mouldings, high ceilings designed with bigger animals in mind. The paint had been applied over and over and layered with fine intermediate coatings of cooking grease. The floors were a dinged-up dead-tree colour, the walls a grey-blue fuzzed with dander.

There was a long hall with a few doorways. Alfonzo imagined a closet, then a bath, then a kitchen behind them. Alfonzo had been in many such apartments over the years. Friends' places growing up. Layouts recycled and reused across the city. He peered into the first open door, expecting to see a small room, maybe a bed or layer of straw, but what he saw instead were cardboard boxes, floor-to-ceiling cardboard boxes in an impressively deranged display. A narrow pathway between the box stacks was the only clear space.

The voice from before beckoned them on into yet another room of boxes. There wasn't much space for Alfonzo and Mitchell to manoeuvre. Besides the boxes, the only thing these hidden inhabitants owned were many large houseplants with nibble-marked leaves. They also had tropical-beach-print towels draped over some larger boxes, creating a network of caves. In some areas of the room, the boxes were arranged according to colour and size. Their obsessiveness translated into decorative pleasure. The boxes were stamped and marked with icons, logos, and names. Yellow fishes, red foxes, paw prints, beavers and seals, stars and moons. ASTRAL PROJECTION PRESS, said one box. Alfonzo read, BORROWED TIMES, DOCK OF THE BAY, THE OCTOPUS, FISH CHEER, KUDZU, and THE GREAT SPECKLED BIRD. Jostling close in the entryway, he and Mitchell looked around for the body attached to the voice.

Alfonzo hummed to Mitchell, "Are these dudes crazy?"

Mitchell hummed back that they could talk about it later.

Mitchell coughed. "If you're busy, I can leave some paperwork and come back when it's more convenient."

All of a sudden two cats appeared. A black-and-white cat sat on top of a box. Alfonzo hadn't seen him jump.

Perched on a lower box was a smaller, beautiful Russian blue wearing a floral scarf. Had they been there the whole time? The animals all stared at one another.

Mitchell finally ventured, "Mr. Stan?"

"Mr. Stan was probably my dad," said the black-and-white cat. "Never met the cat, but I've got to assume he would have liked formalities. Please, call me Tuxedo."

Tuxedo looked adoringly at the Russian blue.

"This is the love of my life, Lipstick Koko."

The cats hopped down and rubbed their faces against Mitchell's and Alfonzo's legs. They behaved as if there were nothing strange going on, and maybe this was normal for them. Alfonzo liked their soft knee-level brushes.

A thing about cats—Alfonzo always thought—was that they liked mixing signals without acknowledging the tension between warmth and aggression. A cat might spend ten minutes glaring from across the bar, then buy you a drink. Or they'd be all jokes at the bodega, only to turn in an instant and streak out the door like the place was on fire. They were delicate.

In college, Alfonzo was housemates with a cat named Norbu, a Siamese from Baltimore who studied linguistics and political science. Nor was a nice cat who'd moved to DC and gotten married after college. Now he had a mortgage, five kittens, and a job with the FCC. But back in college, he and Alfonzo used to smoke catnip together, and when they did they would get into convoluted conversations about animal nature, cat hip-hop, and Egyptian conspiracies.

Alfonzo once asked him to explain the mystery of cats. "Why do cats run so hot and cold? One minute they're purring and acting like your best friend, and the next minute they've run into the nearest closet like you're a monster."

Norbu pointed out, half joking, that these stereotypes were kind of offensive. Then he tried to answer the question seriously, and told Alfonzo something that had lingered with the alpaca ever since. "Look at context. We're small by most measures, but we're trying to make a mark in the world of horses and deer, big dogs, coyotes, and every other kind of dumb hairball who thinks they're King Fuck of Dung Mountain. Think about power, size, and status. Maybe I wouldn't hurt a fly, but do I want my big friends to know that? I've got to keep you off-balance psychologically to protect myself. Like maybe you think you're 'just being friendly,' but you could stomp me by accident. We've got to be constantly aware because we're small."

But Norbu also revealed that sometimes cats were just weirdo fur-brains who liked to mess around: "Just get with cat humour," he advised.

Alfonzo supposed it was wrong to point out one's own view of a different animal's nature—or rather, to project your conceptions of reality onto them, as if what you perceived was objective reality. Alfonzo had tried to accept others as they were, in all their weirdness. He practised the mental gymnastics of putting himself in others' positions. Alfonzo kept telling himself that empathy was an ongoing practice, not a destination.

Mitchell began giving his Office of Affordable Housing spiel. He had a questionnaire. Would they mind answering a few basics about the state of their domicile?

"Not at all," purred the cats.

They went back and forth with yeses and nos, scales of ones to tens, dates and details.

"So, on the phone you told me about some grievances. Have you submitted your complaints in writing to your landlord and given sufficient time for response?"

With this question, Tuxedo started to flick his tail irritably. He became silent.

"Putting things in writing is very important if you want the process to move forward," Mitchell said gently.

"One reason we called you is that we didn't want to put it in writing."

"Language is what defines the process. It's all that anyone counts."

The cats clearly didn't like what they were hearing. Lipstick began to flick her tail in solidarity.

Mitchell attempted to get things back on track. "I can help you write it up. And rest assured that what we discuss here is confidential."

The cats began to purr in a whisper.

"It's all because of the hurricane," said Tuxedo. And with that came a stream of troubles.

The two cats meowed about the night of the storm. They described the hours without light or heat as the building had swayed and they watched wave after massive wave carry away lawn furniture and scooters. It took away cars and houses. It washed away their neighbours, an old dog they knew and a whole family of goats. They had seen it all out their window. They had no radio, no working phone, and no idea how bad things were in the rest of the city. They thought they would die.

Mitchell again pressed for details. Did their landlord's abuse get worse after the storm? Did they have documentation? A paper trail?

Tuxedo had a shoebox of files somewhere. "Well, I did write about the mould of course. But it's not that."

"Really, the landlord is on a campaign to dispose of us, whole cloth," Lipstick said.

"He hates us because we're poor!" Tuxedo meowed.

"Not because we're poor but because we are onto them!" Lipstick added.

"Has your landlord been transparent? Has he threatened you?"

"He's not see-through, if that's what you mean. But no, I kid—he's too savvy to say anything outright. We know because of the holes."

"The holes," Lipstick echoed sadly.

"They're listening in, because of what we've been through. Because of who we know. It's easier to show you."

Lipstick and Tuxedo gestured, so Mitchell and Alfonzo followed. They threaded back through the boxes. The bedroom had dusty, linty pillows and blankets on top of, in, and around more boxes. But behind the boxes was an open space. Everything had been pushed away from the wall. Across its length hung a bright blue tarp. The cats ceremonially pushed it aside, and Tuxedo sat on the plastic that pooled on the floor so that they could get a clear view. The wall was perforated with many small holes.

"We've stuffed them with steel wool and painted them over, but new holes keep appearing," Tuxedo lamented.

"They want us o-u-t because we saw the truth," Lipstick exclaimed.

Lipstick yowled into a hole, "This is harassment, you monsters!"

Alfonzo wondered if all of Mitchell's site visits were like this. He tried to catch his friend's gaze, but Mitchell was taking notes and nodding, as if this were all normal.

"Come," Tuxedo invited. "Examine a hole."

"Well, I don't know if that's necessary." Mitchell kept scribbling.

Lipstick and Tuxedo insisted. So, Alfonzo took the initiative and stepped over. The hole was about the size of a mouse's door, or his own eyeball. Alfonzo bent down and peered in, but all he could see was a bit of plaster, some darkness, and at the far end a pinprick of light. "Take a listen," Tuxedo encouraged. Alfonzo pressed his ear to the wall.

These cats, landlords, Mitchell, I myself, this whole fucking city—we're all crazy, he thought. Alfonzo closed his eyes. At first, he heard nothing but his inner hum. But then— like when you listen to a shell—he heard a whoosh, a tiny roar. There were rumbles and crashes. A sucking-heaving sound.

Maybe this was how you turned crazy. A slow build of anxiety culminating with you standing, ear against the wall, as the old pipes rumbled in a way that makes you think of the encroaching sea. Alfonzo swore he could hear the calls of gulls over a salty burble.

Tuxedo broke the spell. "On top of the Swiss cheesing of the wall, they accuse us of being hoarders. But they're the real sickos here."

"Collecting boxes is not a crime," Lipstick insisted. "But collecting money is."

Alfonzo stretched his neck up. He wanted to be away from this place. Away from the bickering, the depression, and the noise. He looked out the cats' window that framed the sea, a distant band of grey-blue flux under bright sky. The waves rolled in, then pulled back with pretty white ripples. A few gulls skimmed past.

He felt a bump against his leg. Lipstick was again butting her head on his shin. He didn't want to talk, and his head ached. He thought it was clear that Mitchell had this under control.

"My associate is really the one you should be speaking with. I'm afraid this isn't my area of expertise," Alfonzo said.

But the small cat let out a cry, so to be polite Alfonzo leaned down to her level.

"Our friend called you trustworthy. So, we took the risk," she whispered.

"Which friend? What risk?"

"Just a friend."

"I think there's been a misunderstanding. Housing is not my area. I'm here to help Mr. Cusco out—"

"He brought you to hear," Lipstick purred.

"Ma'am, you misunderstand. I can't do anything."

"That's what you think."

Lipstick's fur was up. She struck him as slightly un-glued. Alfonzo worried about what could happen out here on city business that didn't involve him. Had he given his name? What if she called the Hall? What if someone came asking about his presence on a site visit for another department? There were probably confidentiality issues. He tried signalling to Mitchell, but the llama was still locked in a convoluted exchange with Tuxedo.

Lipstick was flicking her tail with great energy. Her purr was aggressive. She whispered, "Arise with the tide," three times like a mantra. Then, with abrupt energy, she bit Alfonzo's ear hard with her pointy little teeth.

He made a lame, high-pitched squawk as he jerked upward in shock. Lipstick's eyes were wide, as if equally amazed by her action and the alpaca's reaction. The cat sprang up with all four legs and tail stiff. She landed noiselessly, then sprinted headlong into a box heap, caus-ing a great hollow clatter of cardboard falling onto card-board. Tuxedo and Mitchell both looked accusingly at Alfonzo. He gaped like a fish, ear smarting.

"My darling? Are you all right?"

They all waited for an answer, but none came. Lipstick was gone. Clouds moved outside the window, and the room darkened. Mitchell waggled his eyebrows at Alfonzo.

"This might be our cue to leave. I want to thank you, Mr. Stan. I appreciate your talking me through your issue. Our office will do some research, and I assure you that your report will remain anonymous. You'll be hearing from me."

14.

"She chomped me!"

The afternoon clouds had melted away, exposing a variegated sky of salmon, orange, and pale yellow. Alfonzo and Mitchell moved in the direction of the subway, but when they got to the entrance they kept walking. Across from them stretched the boardwalk and beyond that the sea. With the slightest hum, they agreed they wouldn't return to the city just yet.

Mitchell shrugged. "I wish I could say that was unusual, but—"

"But what—your clients bite you regularly?"

"Animals get heated when it comes to their homes. It's a sensitive topic. I don't think their fears are unfounded."

"But biting?" Alfonzo huffed. "I didn't do anything to her."

"Everybody bites sometime. Let me buy you a drink to make up for it. I'll tell you some stuff about those cats when the time is right. But now is about getting you through your crisis. How are you feeling, aside from the ear?" Mitchell asked.

Alfonzo felt giddy. He sighed because he could not bear the weight of the day. They scanned for a bar. As far as they could tell, their choices were the Blue Boar Tavern or the Spouter Inn. The Blue Boar looked like it specialized in locally fermented livers. It had one tiny grim window, a closed green door, and a sign that used to spell COORS but had been abbreviated to a simple neon COO. The Spouter, by contrast, had a wide-open door and the Detroit Cobras playing on the stereo.

Alfonzo and Mitchell settled at the counter. They had a view of the street and the sea. The collie behind the bar wagged her tail while taking their orders. Because it was still the afternoon, the place was loose and uncrowded. The staff prepped and gossiped. Alfonzo relished this escape from the nine-to-five bubble.

"Let me give some encouragement," Mitchell began. "First, let's make an inventory. I do little self-assessments when I'm feeling low. It helps. You have a stable job that doesn't require the use of your full intelligence. You have your own apartment in one of the most expensive cities. Granted, it's a dank rat hole, but it's yours. You're devilishly clever. You're friends with me. You are still young. Or at least you're youngish."

Mitchell sounded like he had prepared this speech long ago.

"Be nice."

"That's exactly what I'm doing! Point being, you're not getting your PhD. So what? I think it's a sign from the great cosmic camelid. You're alive and healthy, and there's more to life than the graduate centre."

Guilt shivered through Alfonzo. He was ignoring the positive, he admonished himself. Animals everywhere were dying. They were dying of starvation and poisoning and fighting while he was here, moping about his inability to produce a stellar academic product. He'd inflicted this on himself to avoid the challenges of the real world. Yet that burden was all he had.

"But without a career, what am I? I'm not anybody's mate or parent. I am not even a particularly good son. I'm not politically active. I don't volunteer. I haven't been to a dentist in years. My only hobby is listening to music. You know how it is in this city. It's not enough to just exist. Without a purpose in life, you're just a body taking up space. I feel myself dissolving into my surroundings." He looked at Mitchell and almost hated him for his resilience. He was being such a good friend and Alfonzo was acting like a baby. He could add *bad friend* to his list of descriptors. "And here you've been this whole time doing your job with such conviction. New Yorkers actually need you. But me," Alfonzo scoffed, "I've been going through the motions. I'm a waste of wool."

"Oh, please."

"I had this vision of myself transcending, like, I don't know, my Queens roots? My dad's obsessions? This dumb cartoon version of who we are as a species?"

"For hump's sakes!" Mitchell exclaimed. "You've taught me so much! Stop with this hair shirt mentality. When will you put your learning to use in the world? We're from the Andes! From a proud and noble lineage. We have a gift for walking and carrying, for astronomy, for consensus building. You're the one who told me that our cosmic mother cries rain and our ancient ancestors saved us from that downpour. We can spread the word. We're surrounded by animals who think of us as spitty wool machines! Meanwhile, we have some things to offer!" He took a breath. "We're witnessing our mayor and his cronies turning our city into a shopping centre mixed with a prison. We're surrounded by brilliant animals from all over the world who are forced to act out all these idiotic roles. Who do you know who's able to use their full brilliance? You and I work in the belly of the beast. We went into public service to do good, not to watch it be eaten from within."

Alfonzo cocked his head. It felt like the speech was more about Mitchell than about his academic disaster.

"You think Pamella wants to banter about coffee with Dawn, or with me for that matter? You think what the market wants has anything to do with what the spirit demands? Are we all destined to spend our time filing papers, or spraying whipped cream on mochas, or trading little bits of plastic garbage back and forth?"

Mitchell huffed, embarrassed with himself. That was the gist of it. You lay out all your deepest fears, and it sounds like just another dumb monologue at a bar.

Alfonzo hummed along to the stereo and motioned for another round of whatever the bartender had poured them earlier.

"We are the bureaucrats. We keep this city glued together. We are the glue, but maybe we need to start unsticking ourselves in order to change things! Animals with necessary jobs are devalued, while those who rob the rest of us blind are elevated to guru level. I mean, I expect to hear this nonsense on the news, but from you I expect better. Postal workers, schoolteachers, the MTA maintenance crew, the adorable creature making us coffee, cats fighting their predatory landlord, some sad alpaca who keeps the records of our civilization in order—we're workers. The city needs our intelligence and participation."

"Yes, but—"

"Shut up. Another thing. You've spent all this time romanticizing the university. But it's sick right now. It's not doing what it should be doing. It's infected with the same thing that's infected the state."

"Money."

"Fucking right it's money. They're betraying us, they're stealing our intelligence and our time, they're degrading the necessary tasks we perform. I don't know how to stop it, but I do believe there are more of us than them, and that we have things worth fighting for, even if the struggle has to be done in secret."

Alfonzo hung his head.

"When we murmur low together, when we listen and plan and dream and even just complain together, pockets open, things expand, new possibilities emerge. Just by being together we change the atmosphere. They're trying to make us isolated and alone, but I for one am not going to give in. I just think"—Mitchell searched the ceiling for inspiration—"you need to commit."

"To what?"

"This is your chance. This so-called failure is your opportunity to become some other voice. To speak about the real. We need you writing about stuff that animals care about. You're our great woolly hope."

"Stop!" Alfonzo said, and Mitchell began to laugh like a maniac. He was excited but also drunk. The collie had refilled their glasses a third time without being asked.

Long shadows cut across the beach and spilled into the bar. The edge of the sun was disappearing somewhere down below the sea as "Free Bird" came on the stereo. One of those absurd moments when the cheesy radio feels just right.

"So, what should I do? Turn my dissertation into a book?"

"Who wants that? Do you want that?"

Alfonzo shrugged.

"That project was good practice, but . . ."

"So, you think I should make something new? Like how about a working animal's history?"

"Yawn."

"You mock, but that's what's in my brain."

"I don't know, Al. I think you're at a hinge. Something new is coming, and you just need to ready yourself."

Alfonzo felt compelled to make a joke. "How about I quit Records and get into headlines? I've always loved them."

"Do you really have what it takes?"

"Sure, I am willing to devote myself to becoming the best at puns—I'll remake myself into a regular punisher, if you will."

"But you'd be under a lot of pressure. You'd have to handle a wide variety of stories."

"Try me. Give me a subject."

"Bear mental health crisis."

"Easy. 'Bipolar De-fur-al,' 'Trans-fur-ance,' something something."

"You're not convincing me."

"Give me another."

"Okay, the paper needs a snappy headline about a literacy program aimed at snakes."

"Umm, 'Reading Rainboa'?"

"That's bad, but also kind of good."

"This is just me warming up. Stop insulting my puns or alpaca my things and go."

"Weren't you considering suicide before? Maybe we should revisit that. Remember the whole jokey thing the *Post* did on that bird Yvonne who got lost out in Jamaica Bay?"

"On the plastic raft? What a saga."

"Poor Yvonne, jerk chicken of the sea."

They got the giggles so bad that the animals around the bar started giving them looks. Alfonzo huffed and hummed to calm down.

By now it was fully dark outside. The bar had come to life as waves of animals crowded in post-work. There was no room to move. The bartender had gotten fresh assistance in the form of two crow servers who carried wooden trays on cords around their necks. They hopped back and forth across the bar, distributing glasses, returning with empties. The demand was constant. No sooner had they alighted than the bartender was loading up their trays with fresh drinks. She garnished cocktails with sprigs of grass or splashed them with tuna juice; she opened bottles of Dogs Head beer and poured glasses of Yellow Tail at a dizzying pace.

In pausing, it hit Alfonzo how far they were from home and how drunk they were. His head spun.

Mitchell leaned over. "There was something I've been wanting to tell you."

"Unless it has to do with getting home or eating pizza, I don't think I'm in any state to process."

"Okay, another time."

"You want to spring for a taxi?"

"What are we, Rockefellers?"

They stumbled into the night and toward the subway.

15.

At home, headachy after the half-drunk hysterical euphoria, Alfonzo riffled through his bag in search of ibuprofen. He couldn't locate the pills, but he did find a mysterious little blue book.

He recognized the name from that afternoon, *Borrowed Times*, written above the logo of a striped fish. It must have come from the cats' apartment. Sprawling on the floor, he leafed through it. It was a crude publication without pictures or much information as to who produced it. It had only a cryptic text on the back inside cover.

> Produced by Friends of SERF (Sea
> Equality Revolutionary Front). F-SERF is
> a society of land creatures dedicated to
> furthering the cause of sea liberation by
> any and all means.

The printing was a little blurry, and the pamphlet reminded him of the hard-core zines of his youth. He liked documents like this: subcultural, self-produced work. It felt a little dangerous or at least a swerve away from adulthood.

He started at the beginning.

History
We came from the sea.

Our ancient selves were aquatic. Life on land only began with a valiant crawl by fin upward. Sea and land were always family.

Family may scatter, but all honoured sea womb. Remember salt-lick snot of mothers and mothers' mothers?

We maintained ties. Family was family was family.

Those who moved to land kept the sea inside alive. Ancient ancestors painted shells and wave forms; they carved fish shapes and dolphin profiles in bas-relief. Ocean gods were equal to other deities. Water prayers were pounded out with hooves, and villages were built in spirals, like shells. Communities grew like coral.

This relationship between wet and dry went on for millennia.

Gradually, though, those on land began to deny their sea roots. They grew arrogant and thought they were the creators of all. They forgot the sea mothers, as if a sky father alone could birth you.

The landed decided the sea was foreign space. They forgot the means of communication and wondered if our sea others even knew how to speak or think. They threw letters in bottles into the sea. They gave speeches and sang. Then another land war began.

In war, land creatures had to entrust themselves to ships they'd built. They spent months sailing and came down with scurvy and mange. Plague travelled in fleas. When the sailor warriors got to shore they jumped into the business of biting and scratching, mauling and kicking, all the while spreading their diseases. Wars are a dirty business.

In that time of war and plunder, many filled ships were lost. Seafarers who survived told ghastly tales of storms and drowning.

Thinkers and politicians developed new anti-sea ideas. It became easier to blame whatever lay unknown beneath the waves than to look hard at what they were creating.

Philosophers began to argue for a hierarchy of existence, with the sea at the bottom. "Who has rightful dominion?" asked those who presumed that dominion was already theirs. "What does it mean to breathe? Who has feelings?" Scholars taught classes on classification and standardization.

Then came yet another age, yet another spirit.

There was gold to be mined, and silver, diamonds, copper, and tin. Oil to drill for.

Coffee, nuts, and fruits to be harvested. Wood to be cut. Kings, slave drivers, capitalists, and militaries ground animals into nothing, into bone piles.

The ancient excretions of the sea were no longer sacred. The land animals grabbed all the guano they could carry. Ancient waste was mined and spread, killing the living in the process. But this shit-gold turned deserts into new Edens of blossom, fruit, and nuts. So, they thought all the blood was worth it. We wouldn't have modernity without artificial seabird shit.

Invasive populations exploded with a great squealing sound in clouds of feather and fur. Then came general disorder. Everyone was effulgent except the workers, who coughed with black, brown, with guano lung and coal lung, with wet lung and silica lung. The workers' life expectations were kept low.

Ancient History

So much has changed and yet so little too.

Land society has undergone massive transformations. Packs of determined creatures have clawed rights from the ruling classes. Whole societies and small groups have argued and gnawed innovations into existence. We made life better and came to believe democracy was possible.

But the struggle has been fierce, and some might say we have fallen backward, even as the good that surrounds us has become ever shinier and ever more chewable, ever softer and ever more transfixing.

Everyone is making, buying, and using plastic and oil. Industry is visible in the exploded view. See the guts of the machine and rejoice. We breathe particles and eat microflecks. Now we sit in cramped cat cafés eating tuna from cans. We are post-industry now, they crow, yet so many of us are still busy making industries run.

Lead pipes still carry our water. Styrofoam bowls that held our kibble fly free from dump trucks. Dye baths in clothing factories flow toward the oceans, turn rivers foamy red, pink, and green in the process. Tanks, cars, trucks, and boats, septic ranches and sepsis farms, leak themselves into the sea. Imagine millions of motor engines dripping a drop of oil each day onto roads and parking lots. All that mixes and flows into the sea. Chemicals travel great distances and accumulate in marine life. All this waste finds its way back to us.

While the most visible forms of our destruction are catastrophic spills, avalanches, fires, and explosions, those are minor in comparison and serve as spectacles to obscure the greater violence of the unspectacular. Shards, flecks, dribbles, and specks are what we wish to forget. What's really destroying us is this slow carcinogenic drip. It comes from everywhere. What you can't see is more dangerous than what you can.

We have long since forgotten our link to the sea.

Near Future

We are a coalition started in the seaside city of industry and money. Now we span the globe in an invisible web. We are linked by boats and belief. From our vantage, we have seen the ups and downs of the system and the tides. The clear-headed among us see a connection.

We have been treating the ocean like a garbage dump, and it has been taking it for a long time. But there are so many signs that this cannot continue.

Storms are coming, and they threaten all of us. Yet the captains of industry do not care. They are busy fashioning mountaintops into bunkers in which they will retreat while the rest of us drown.

The problems are tidal waves coming one after another.

So, what do we do?

Bury our heads in the wet sand?

Curl into a ball so that our tails cover our eyes as the waves break?

NO!

We, the creatures of today, the Friends of SERF, will act.

We are rising up and spreading truth!

We ask you to join this survival struggle. When the time comes to act out, you will know. You will know when you know the sea inside your soul!

In the meantime, forward with the struggle for clean water, strong nature, and a unified animalism! Be open and friendly to your friends. Listen for the water to communicate its truths. To you.

Let us rise with the tides and move with the SERF!

MACHINES OF
LOVING GRACE

16.

It was some Tuesday morning tucked in the folds of November. A weekday bathed in the weak light of fall. Alfonzo trudged up the gunky subway stairs.

A strong wind busied itself rifling through the contents of City Hall's park. Alfonzo crossed the street. Got a coffee without making a joke or exchanging words with Pamella beyond "Americano" and "Thank you." He did not linger on his bench or watch the tourists waiting for their tour guide. He went straight to the basement.

The Department of Records existed. The department was open Monday to Friday, 9:00 a.m. to 5:00 p.m. The department rustled with paper. It accumulated dust that needed to be swept. The floors were concrete, the walls brick, the shelves wood. The temperature was controlled. The air was central. Water pooled, and he was there to mop up the puddles. City Hall existed. Alfonzo gave it that, though it was all he could give.

Information scientists had long ago devised and adapted systems of organization to keep collections useful. Animals like Alfonzo—not an expert, just a cog— were tasked with bringing these systems to life. He himself was not empowered to officially change what he worked within. Any adaptation he introduced was private, an unofficial quirk or a workaround; on the record his variations didn't exist, so they didn't exist. Whatever flair he had could be swept away like the dust bunnies. But on paper and therefore in some version of reality, Alfonzo's position within records existed, so his body showed up to fill it.

For much of Alfonzo's life, this routine of filling an available space for pay had comforted him. "Come and repeat," the city said, so he did. Rhythm was comfort. But ever since Vinograd, rhythm had become a suffocating constraint. He was just another rat in the nest, just one more bat within the castle. Wind whistled in the pneumatic tubes, whistled for his soul. The enclosure promised all its creatures, "You are safe within me, you are protected here, but you must never leave."

He unlocked the basement door, negotiating his body through the dark. He turned on his small lamp, which gave just enough light to despair to, and slumped down behind his desk.

Alfonzo never used the overhead fluorescents if he could help it. They emitted an almost inaudible, yet horrid, buzzing. They also intensified the wall colour, a green-grey-rust shade called Industrial Catbabble. The floors and ceiling were a beige-mauve-aqua called Skink. Alfonzo knew the paints' official names from reading Department of Maintenance files. He knew the city had purchased fifteen thousand gallons from a company called Gold Brush—a company that just happened to be owned by Mayor Shergar's college roommate.

Alfonzo theorized that the higher-ups had chosen these specific colours not just because of the company's ties but also because they drained animals' spirits. He felt sure the mayor wanted city workers floppy and despondent. Some psychologist could prove this if he or she ever took the time to study paint. "Guilt, Authority, and Chromatics: A Study of the Effects of Paint Hue on Mammal Desolation." He would read that paper. Or maybe these were simply the random colours that came from mixing the leftovers of all other colours. Either the city wanted to crush workers or the crushing was an unintended consequence of cost saving. Anything was possible.

His neck ached, and it was only 9:18 a.m.

Somewhere upstairs, an assistant was placing a rye latte with organic oat milk on the mayor's desk. Various phones were ringing. Someone answered a call and jotted down a request. "The deputy will get back to you." She stuffed the note into the appropriate message cubby. Through the hallways scurried assistants, council members, and interns. In a chamber outside the bullpen, an undersecretary for public communications was speaking to reporters on the city beat. "The press conference will begin shortly," he barked. "The mayor is just running a touch late." Upstairs it was business as immutable.

Alfonzo contemplated work. He should do some. That was what he was here for, after all. He lifted his head and began to examine the day's folders in his wire-basket inbox. There was the fire incident dispatch data from the last quarter, August's facades-compliance filings, a report on boiler safety, and the directory of teachers' pension fund financial reports. His toes clattered the keys of his machine as he entered his first code of the day, 7–2–4–1–7–8–3-c-v.

His hunched body felt dwarfed yet unwieldy. The furniture surrounding him towered and perched, shelves too tall and chairs too small. The only object his size was the Aztek Howtek. It sat cold and silent in the corner.

Alfonzo typed slowly for the next hour. He just about finished a single task. His neck, ankles, and stomach ached. Pain roamed freely through his body, around his shoulders, up his neck and back down. He ached and twisted. Bits of him went to sleep, then awoke pinned and needled. How had he ever written a whole dissertation? It seemed ludicrous now, though it hadn't been so long ago. How had he learned to type? Middle school technology class was the literal answer, but Alfonzo's question was more metaphysical. How did his brain trace through to his limbs? He watched himself as he hunted-and-pecked the next code. 7–1–5–1–8–9–2-b-g.

How does an animal type? Move your toes one at a time, but quick. Remember the pattern or just feel the alphabet out of order. Setting his attention straight meant losing his body's confidence. He used the keyboard every day, but he could not tell where the letters fell. *A* was beside *S*, and the space bar stretched the bottom.

How did he write? Alfonzo puzzled. How did he form words, even, let alone strings of words that he wove into blankets of thought? It didn't make sense when he thought about it, yet language was what supposedly distinguished him from fishes.

Alfonzo no longer felt like a thinking creature. He was growing dumb, or maybe had always been. What was he good for but carrying bits of paper back and forth? He was a pack animal, after all.

Alfonzo turned off his emotional self and began to type away at great speed. His keyboard let Alfonzo's codes flow through it. Animal and object gave in to the thoughtless repetition. This was supposed to be useful. The paperwork pile shrank, then rose again as more files arrived from the singing tubes. This was what he was paid for. He typed and he filed. The process was so rhythmic it drowned out thought. He became a smooth surface.

At 5:18 p.m., Alfonzo returned to himself. He turned off his machines, switched the basement dark, locked the door, and wandered up into the world.

The city had just emerged from a late-afternoon shower in time for sunset. Water drops slicked the navy awning of a salad bar. Long fall rays slanted across wet-paper-bag leaves. The city was preparing for a night of drinking and flirting.

Alfonzo decided to unwind by walking home. He hadn't crossed the Brooklyn Bridge in a dog's age. The after-work herd gave him a sense of dissolving. Delivery creatures pinged along the bike lanes. Birds flew just overhead wearing tiny messenger bags. Sheep in neckties and dogs in coats stepped along beside anxious raccoons pushing strollers. Was it so bad to be a herd animal? In this together, carrying our loads.

He passed the Seafarers Institute with its sentinel line of statues. The bear and the eagle peered out from the rooftop. He'd learned during his research that these statues had been put there to greet arriving ships. Alfonzo felt not that the city was a port, but that the whole of New York was its own kind of vessel, one that stayed in one place but rocked continually.

He crossed onto one of the bridges that roped boroughs together.

In his research, he had learned that the Andean ancestors had erected pillars on the mountain peaks and hills to create a huge sun clock. They had laid out their whole built environment to mirror their map of the cosmos. Each time the sun aligned with one of the pillars, the ancient animals knew it was time to plant or harvest, sacrifice or dance. They embedded symbols of the astral plane into their buildings. Midway across the bridge, he turned to look back to Manhattan. The skyline was dotted with gargoyles, cupolas, signs, water towers, and sheer cliffs of glass. The setting sun turned everything gold and shadowy.

Strolling reminded Alfonzo of how much school had taken from him, how much work had been done at the expense of living life.

The water moved beneath. He looked down, then onward to Dumbo. He threaded his way into Brooklyn Heights. The street lights were on, illuminating parents and their young meandering toward dinner. He passed a horse carrying both her work bag and her foal's fish-shaped backpack. The child clipped along, chattering joyfully.

Alfonzo passed finally into what he considered the boundaries of his own neighbourhood of Gowanus. Like most of Brooklyn, it was mutating, or experiencing a kind of trauma. Every week an old store closed and a more expensive version replaced it. A popular no-frills Siamese cat restaurant had disappeared, and in its place came a fine-dining street-food spot with dim lights and rope-decorated walls. Across the street, an old-fashioned grooming parlour called You Have Nails had been supplanted by a barber shop run by rugged bandana-wearing dogs. It was a process of repetition and replacement with difference, where the main difference was always price.

Animals who'd been forced out of their dens in other neighbourhoods came to a new area. The locals grumbled, and the arrivistes felt wounded. They'd only moved out to Brooklyn because they could no longer afford Manhattan. Furious creatures organized meetings. Aggrieved animals wrote op-eds and occasionally attacked one another. The mayor said the lack of affordable apartments was actually a good thing. Residents without millions asked, "But where the hell are we supposed to dwell?"

The song played on repeat. Samples found their way into joints that played on Hot 97. These songs were sung in every language of New York. The din was so constant it felt redundant to mention it. Or rather, everyone discussed these issues so constantly that outrage and criticism became just an undertone of the general hum.

The whole city danced to the sounds of disappearing habitat.

Mitchell and Alfonzo had grown up in the bad old days, during New York's last bout of mange. The number of times teenage Alfonzo had had scraggly dudes try to psych him out, rob him, or just bite him for fun was beyond counting. And that was everyone's experience. His mom, his dad—all his family, really—had been mugged or had had their house broken into at one time or another. His dad's car windows had been smashed multiple times. Mitchell had been jumped by a gang of dogs in school. He'd had to have stitches. "It's just normal," everyone agreed. But still, the ambient violence of the old city made everyone obsessed with not getting "played out."

But then, as they'd matured, those grungy, sometimes thrilling neighbourhoods were slowly transformed by the arrival of bank branches, chain pharmacies, lamb boutiques, and Buffalo Wild Wings.

"What can you do?" everyone sighed. "If you don't like change, you don't like New York."

Was the only choice between real and stressful threat or getting slowly expelled because of price? It felt like a false choice, but it was a false choice playing out in concrete and chains, block by block.

Gowanus fluctuated between life and poison, attractor and repellant. Some city moguls had hired packs of builders to erase lifetimes' worth of associations between the canal and industrial putrefaction. In some office in Manhattan, no doubt, a team of dogs and monkeys was trying out alternative names for this tract of waterfront land, something like Park Slope River or GoCa. Their job was tricky because *Gowanus* and *Canal* contained both *anus* and *anal*. It was a little on the nose for that body of water. But hey, Alfonzo mused, for many animals a good butt sniff could be a selling point.

When Alfonzo moved to Gowanus his neighbours had been a garage, a casket-making company, and a coyote social club. The dusty local park was populated by punk pigeons and gulls. There had been a squat on Third and Third. Neighbours resigned themselves to their monster canal that foamed with sewage when it rained. They accepted it was probably killing them. Still, the area had been cozy in a blighted way: the coyote social club members slunk in and out quietly, the raccoon grandmothers kept well-maintained outdoor religious displays in front of their buildings, and the seagulls hanging out wisecracked democratically.

But he should have known something was up when the squatted building was designated historic. It had been an MTA powerhouse during the Herbert era, but that was ages ago. As far as Alfonzo had ever known, it was the straight-edge squat known as the Bat Cave. The frontage was marked by a big piece of graffiti, a painting of a spiderweb with the threads spelling out the word: radiant. One day, police came and evicted the squatters. Then workers came and fenced it off. The building was put on the market and sold for an astronomical sum. It was slated to become an arts centre redesigned by famous architects. "They" were going to preserve the graffiti.

Before home, Alfonzo stopped at the fancy grocery

store that had opened as part of the local transformation. He often shopped there, and felt ashamed and annoyed every time he did. But he was craving Bermuda grass and clover and cilantro and parsley. He also wanted those special Mauri Alpaca chews they didn't have anywhere else. He ogled the dewy produce and inhaled the store's consistent odour of lavender and lemongrass. A cashmere goat browsed while her free-range kids bounced around like popping corn. A chow chow blocked the aisle with her little wheeled basket full of wild-caught sardines and natural peanut butter.

Leaving the store, Alfonzo noticed something off in the canal. There was an industrial sucking noise, and the multicoloured dome that was some kind of public art was disappearing beneath the surface of blue-black-grey, rust-coloured foam. A few months back, the store had unveiled this floating sculpture. It was meant to spruce up the arsenic-infused water. The artist had made a geodesic globe out of recycled umbrellas. You got a good view of the piece while sitting on the store's benches. Alfonzo and Mitchell had mocked it many times while eating salads from the buffet. What an absurd ornament to decorate the ass water.

But something had caught hold since his last visit. The Gowanus would not let art disturb its chemical death. The spindly orb was almost fully submerged, and as Alfonzo stood on the dark walkway, the last bit of the globe sucked beneath the water's surface. He looked around for another witness. In the dark sat one of the gutter punk rats from the old squat. They nodded to each other. No matter what the grocery store or the developers wanted, the canal had been there first. It had a stronger will. Industrial toxins would not surrender that easily. The repressed was still there, tugging at the loose edges, testing for the hidden weaknesses.

17.

Rain pattering outside the apartment woke Alfonzo. It was Saturday. He hadn't set an alarm. He couldn't fall back asleep, so he lay in his straw, humming along with the weather and contemplating the state of things.

Since Vinograd, he'd been weepy and easily irritated. He could trick himself into feeling good for little bursts, but most of his waking hours were a blur of despair.

He spent most of his leisure hours lying on his apartment floor. Waves of anxiety rolled in and broke on the shores of his skull in a froth, only to reconstitute again far out in a fresh grey heave. After each crash, he struggled for breath. The next rush always came in too fast. His apartment reflected his interior.

Alfonzo's apartment was a long, narrow rectangle on the first floor of a four-storey walk-up. Its thin taupe walls were filled with off-the-books mouse apartments. The landlord was dipping into two markets at once without maintaining the building for either the large or the small tenants. Sometimes Alfonzo toyed with filing a complaint with Mitchell's office, but he was no snitch.

The studio apartment acted as amplifier both for outside street noise and for the mouse music and chatter inside. Exhaust from the auto body shop next door mixed with grease from the upstairs dogs' cooking. Alfonzo avoided cooking any of his own foods because the smell clung to his belongings. He made coffee and ate cold grass at home. The only reason he had stayed so long was that the rent had never risen. The cheapness held him captive. This was his stall, his solitary cell, his space pod. When Alfonzo lay flat on the floor, which he often did, his woolly brown body filled the room like a nut in its shell.

He used to keep things tidy. He had tried to keep hay fresh and dishes washed. He'd once acquired a lemon candle to banish the musty air. But as soon as he stopped fighting, slum nature took over. His apartment's set point was squalid and dank; if he shirked his duties, even for a moment, the apartment returned to its natural state.

Dust bunnies leapt with the draft that entered through the crack under the front door. Green mould covered the bathroom. The drain was clogged with wool, so every time he ran the taps, murky old water bubbled up from a mysterious below. He had to shower with shoes on.

Roaches came and went like the hooligans they were. His mouse neighbours tapped on the walls. They threw regular parties, and he didn't have the strength to protest.

Alfonzo might have lain on the floor all day, but the phone rang. Alfonzo picked up. What else was he going to do?

"It's your father," said his father. "Will you come out for breakfast? It's been a while."

Alfonzo had been avoiding Luis because he would

have to tell him of the dissertation debacle. But how long could he last without seeing his only living parent?

He trotted through the rain, regretting his clothing. The train was just leaving when he arrived at the subway, and the next train took its sweet time. He stood with dripping wool while animals with umbrellas and coats gathered alongside him on the platform.

Once safely on the train, he pulled an art journal from his bag. He skimmed the table of contents sleepily until one title caught his eye, an excerpt from a book called *Sign/Wave*.

"NOTHING IS AS BEAUTIFUL AS INVOLUNTARY RESEMBLANCE"

Oxana Tennisracket

The fish's unlimited limits make visible the cosmos's abstract machinery. The fish is a positive example of the ontology of affirmation, the very model for becoming, bringing it from the bottom to the apex of the philosophical universe.

All schools are simultaneously collectives and individual beings. One fish makes itself a line in the water. All these lines fit together in an abstract, ever-changing puzzle. A single fish line is made by following other lines, and it is by fitting with others that fish's worlds intersect transparently. Fishes belong to schools as we do to herds or packs.

Fish become imperceptible in water like cats in grass. The abstract marks on a fish's skin resemble nothing but organized disorganization, and yet they are perfectly in sync with their universe of veined rocks, rippled sand, and plant fronds.

Each particle of matter contains a multitude, a garden, a sea full of life. Therefore, there is nowhere uncultivated, not on land nor in the sea. There is nothing dead; there is nowhere wild. No being is unworthy or lesser.

They inhabit another world that swirls alongside ours but is separated by a thin sheath, which is everything. We die when we plunge into their world. They die when they are pulled into ours. We look in this mirror and are terrified, so we choose to twist our fear into hatred.

The earth and seas warm because of an accumulation of gases that raise the temperature of the lower atmosphere. Heat is the transfer of internal kinetic energy; the total energy within a system remains constant. So, what we call heating is actually movement. Particles moving more and more rapidly. The accumulation of gases corresponds to our extraction of earth matter: oil, phosphorous, and precious metals. Our work extracts materials that heat up our world. This is not the work whales and fish do.

If everything on Earth were in harmony, we would not need self-consciousness. We could inhabit the land, and they the water. It is only because the system is untenable that our received wisdom must be torn apart. I would argue that our culture has condemned the sea because sea creatures resist the logic of accumulation. If we were happy and healthy in our living conditions, in our essence, we would not turn on those in the sea. Life would be as transparent as sea water.

However, we workers are not content. We feel our essence only because it is being destroyed. We are like fish who have realized we live in water only because that substance has been filled with poisons.

The uneasiness of a single creature in the world is a problem not only for that creature but also for the world itself, insofar as it has become unbearable. We with paws and claws scoff at the notion of a fish-led revolution. Yet we do not know if we can lead one either. We must trace a line we do not know the shape of; we must become this unknown line within our bodies.

"Mr. Faca, how have things been with you?"

Alfonzo slid into his dad's booth at the Libertad Diner. Dolly, the round sheep waitress who looked the same as all the other waitresses who'd ever worked here, was chatting with Luis.

"I'd complain," he sighed, "but who'd listen?"

Dolly bleated indulgently. Her wool was clean white, like a cotton swab. She nodded, and a department-store rose smell wafted over the table. Luis ordered half a grapefruit for Alfonzo without consultation.

"I want something else, Dad."

"What? You want scurvy?"

"That's a pirate's disease." Alfonzo asked Dolly for a bowl of alfalfa meal and a coffee.

"I apologize for my son—he doesn't care about vitamin C."

"Don't worry about it, Mr. Faca," said Dolly.

Luis never hesitated to sacrifice his son's autonomy in an effort to get some attention. Or maybe this was just another example of his dad's compulsion to be in control. Alfonzo inhaled slowly. *Be nice, he's old.*

"So, have you heard what's happening with the Hole?" Luis asked while skimming the paper.

"No, Dad, where would I hear?"

"No need to be difficult. I thought you might talk to your cousins even when you're avoiding me."

"What's happening with the Hole, Dad?"

The Hole was one of Luis's obsessions.

In strict geographic terms, the Hole was a little triangle of streets stuck between Lindenwood, Howard Beach, and Ozone Park. The ground there was sunk below the surrounding areas because the city had never installed proper sewage and drainage—hence the name. It was a bowl that filled with water whenever it rained. Forgotten animals, outcasts, elderly immigrants, and those on the run lived there. Its most infamous residents were the Federation of Wild Urban Cows and some off-the-grid horses. Asphalt sagged and concrete buckled there—more, that is, than in other neighbourhoods. Birds with broken wings hobbled along the streets. A few film-school nerds had made a documentary about the wild atmosphere of the neighbourhood. It was one of those areas where received real estate wisdom did not apply. Luis wanted it to fit a narrative. Chaos maddened him.

There had been repeated pushes to modernize the Hole. They faltered, came to nothing. Projects went there to die. A few seasons back, someone had started building a condo in the area. Luis said, "Finally," to his friends. But then, amid whispers of shell companies, tax write-offs, and maybe mafia involvement, the builders stopped showing up, and all that was left was a half-built steel husk at the end of Ruby Street. One day Luis made Alfonzo walk over there. His father glowered at the geometry of the steel beams wrapped in decaying blue tarps that flapped like torn sails in the wind. Metaphysically, the Hole was more proof for Luis's belief that goodness and order were contingent and fragile. Luis would only ever tell stories that supported such a view. Bad luck prowled the Hole.

"Mrs. Gustavito," Luis explained, speaking of his very old hippo neighbour with a skin disorder who'd terrified Alfonzo as a child, "was strolling in the Hole last week, minding her own business. Then, *bam*, she was hit by a flying board from that junk heap."

Hippo struck with airborne junk. Alfonzo kept his face straight for his father's sake. "Oh my gosh."

"And then—she didn't want to go to the hospital because she doesn't have insurance. Our other neighbour, that possum nurse, gave her stitches off the books."

"Will she survive?" Alfonzo was sure she would, but he didn't want to deny his father the pleasure of his histrionics.

"This is what happens when you leave politics to nonruminants," Luis grumbled. He could always find a way to steer any conversation toward digestion. "I know you're tired of me bringing this up, but it bears repeating," he said, chewing with emphasis.

"It's not horses I'm against, mind you, just speed. Always want to do everything quick. They give out building permits willy-nilly and then, *bam*, Mrs. Gustavito is brought down by insulation."

"I don't think the mayor gives out building permits."

"It's just . . . I think the city could do a whole lot worse than having a cow, a llama, or maybe even an alpaca as mayor."

"Maybe one day Mitchell will run. I'll be his campaign manager."

His father snorted. "Mitch wouldn't be half bad. You, though, may not be cut out for that level of intensity."

Alfonzo sipped his coffee. The waitress Dolly brought him his bowl of alfalfa meal. It was warm and pleasantly mushy. He made sure to chew slowly. *There is no right time*, Alfonzo thought.

"I've got some bad news to share. My dissertation was rejected."

Luis put down his paper. His fur looked thin and grey. The bell on the diner door clinked as some ox firefighters came in. It was difficult, but verbalizing his disappointment to his father was also a relief.

"Dr. Vinograd thought it was too long. He was right. Maybe there *is* such a thing as too much thinking."

His father looked aghast. Alfonzo interrupted himself with a new rush of self-recrimination. He unspooled all the things he imagined Luis wanted to say. The academy was never meant for him. He should have listened. He should have gone to dental school.

"Don't worry, I'm going to devote myself to work now. I'm going to try to piece together a respectable life. I'm sorry I'm such a disappointment. I'm sorry I failed."

"They're crazy," his father growled. "They wouldn't know smarts if it spit in their eye."

"They don't seem to recognize their lack of recognition, Dad."

"I know your mother loved that you were a scholar. She was so proud, no matter what." Luis coughed and looked up at the ceiling. "I'm no good at this."

Alfonzo stared at his father's half-eaten grapefruit until it vibrated.

Mitchell and Alfonzo had tickets for the Akida Kombu show that night. The llama promised it would be good for Alfonzo's depression to shoot the breeze, listen to a genius, maybe smoke some ciggies afterward.

"Cigarettes obviously aren't good for you, but spiritually isn't it better to smoke with friends than to eat carrots by yourself?"

"Who says I want to live long anyway?"

"Attaboy."

They debated bars. Wolf Whistle used to be good until it was discovered by actual wolves; all those claws and teeth made Alfonzo nervous. He suggested Sun Bear, but according to Mitchell it had closed, supposedly because the landlord jacked the rent. The place was now dark, with a torn FOR LEASE sign on the door. A shame. The Dark Ship was workable for a couple of beers. The White Rabbit might be good for after.

"Lots of snuggling in the dark corners," Alfonzo objected.

The Rusty Knot was around the corner from Vivi and Alfonzo's old apartment.

"Too many memories."

"You're picky. We simply need somewhere near the venue."

They settled on the Hawk and Eagle Tavern, which looked much the same as all the other places but was quieter. Its only downside was his suspicion they were getting charged inflated mammal prices, but that had to be stomached.

Inside the wood-panelled room, surrounded by birds who ignored them, Mitchell regaled Alfonzo with Kombu mythology.

The dog musician recorded prolifically but rarely performed anywhere. This was due, they said, to the strain of sea travel from his island, but it must have also had to do with the politics of the sea. Kombu was a high-profile pro-sea land mammal. The last time Kombu had come to North America, animal control detained him at the port of entry for weeks. According to reports, this was because of visa issues, but his fans knew SERF sympathies made Kombu a target for harassment. In an interview, the dog intimated he'd been forced to sign a document promising that while in the country he would only play music. No "political activism" would be tolerated.

"What's absurd," Mitchell hummed, "is this fantasy that the disasters on his island could ever be excised from his creative work."

Alfonzo was excited. He knew Kombu's recordings. *Koko* and *Le Bruit et l'odeur* were masterpieces that expanded the scope of what music could be.

A crowd had already filled the club by the time Alfonzo and Mitchell arrived. These young creatures brushed against one another in the dim expanse of T-shirts and plain workwear, even though most probably held post-industrial service jobs.

They were assembled to experience sonic pain within the safety of a herd. They were there to bask in the music made by machines not working, or working only to make noise. The crowd came to feel its own wildness. The animals were hushed and heaving. Something secret was about to commence.

Mitchell and Alfonzo hummed as they sipped their grass beers, waiting.

"You know who's a good boy?" Mitchell asked.

Alfonzo rolled his eyes. "Who?"

"You are."

"Thanks, smartass."

A great whistling announced the appearance of Kombu. Alfonzo and Mitchell craned their necks to see the famous dog and his panda drummer. The musicians arranged themselves before a little stand covered with wires and homemade instruments, and when it was clear they were about to begin, the room hushed.

The musicians began to play with electricity, with repurposed machines that were not originally instruments. They began at a deafening intensity and climbed from there. It became so loud that whatever they were making no longer felt like sound. It had grown into something like an enclosure, a din hut. The audience huddled together within this shelter of sound. Alfonzo hummed. Shelter in place. But the waters were rising.

Kombu communed with machines and let them freely express their machinic natures. His instruments roamed landscapes of pink-and-white fuzz; gnashing, repetitive static; and deep purple tones. He built long-duration auditory phenomena with static electricity discharge and temple bells. It was feral music; it scavenged outside the known categories. His oily slick, lightly haired music flopped beneath sonic snow that fell copiously amid spacious ballads sung by repurposed sonar machines. The music served salt-and-pepper coils and cosmic microwave backgrounds sprinkled with a few seconds of birdsong fed through heavy effects pedals.

The panda strummed on springs and rattled an empty tuna can. The dog manipulated fuzz and distortion pedals with his paws. The two musicians were nudging every animal in the room toward an edge. The set moved along with atonal romance. This was beauty from the most hopeless hope-filled mental space.

The sound was a shelter, but it was also the storm. The

sound was the ocean and its waves. Microtones tossed and rose and fell on the surface of deep sound.

Alfonzo felt like a cup floating and filling, floating and being filled with intense longing. Did that mean he was empty? He was. The sounds grew louder still. He sweated. His heart raced. His eyes felt hot. He felt glad it was dark and no one could see. He had entered his own interior, where he could feel the chaotic vulnerability that he would not otherwise touch.

The crowd swayed. They glowed with inchoate hope. They let themselves be pummelled by noise that was being made not with malice but as a tool of transformation. Every animal in the room was there to be beaten by sonic waves and then to emerge. So many needed to feel this screaming. They needed to feel it but could not let out what they were feeling without help. These musicians were the help. Alfonzo loved the herd. They were in this together.

Kombu and Panda kept up their non-violent assault. Their music stormed and crashed but not against anyone; instead it enveloped them all in shared and shifting depths, swells, and tides of feeling. They called out a desire for survival. Microphones, amplifiers, walls of speakers turned this desire collective.

At the end, the great noise ceased, and all that remained was the finest strand of notes. It was a beautiful melody from babyhood, tinkling like a music box. They all breathed together. The whole room. A long silence elapsed, and then everyone, with teary eyes, began yelping and clapping in gratitude. They had made it to some other side.

Alfonzo and Mitchell went to smoke in the cool outdoors. The evening expanded and compressed like a set of lungs. Underneath the streets the city's juices flowed. A vent exhaled a wet, fungal sigh.

18.

Alfonzo woke with a ball of burnt-tasting leaves in his cheek. It was Thursday. He shook the straw from his face. He put on a blue tie, a holey sweater, and a bucket hat.

The clouds were on the verge of snowing or sleeting; they were only trying to decide. Alfonzo scurried through the geometry of commuting: door to subway, subway to café, café to basement.

Alfonzo unlocked his office door and slid into his Catbabble Skink–hued cave. It smelled pungent and damp. He arranged coffee, apple, and paper within his lamp's circle. Alfonzo did not so much read the paper before him as let headlines shimmer into his consciousness.

WHO PAYS FOR CONTAMINATION?

OFFICER PEPE RAT KILLED BY FELLOW RAT
   IN THE LINE OF DUTY

SHERGAR ADMINISTRATION SET TO END
   PROTECTIONS FOR WETLANDS IN A
   VICTORY FOR DEVELOPERS

Upstairs, an assistant was removing a half-drunk coffee from the mayor's desk. Deputies, assistants, and interns scurried through the hallways. Various phones rang on various desks. Someone answered a call, and someone else made one. Some pig composed a memo. Another memo, typed up by another secretary in a different department, sat on a desk. The pig finished, sealed his memo in an envelope, and then deposited it into the nearest pneumatic tube. The envelope disappeared with a whoosh into the singing metallic pipes.

Alfonzo folded his newspaper, then opened the pneumatic duct. Files and envelopes avalanched down into the wire basket. The last piece to fall out was Lenny Old Spots's memo, so Alfonzo saw it right away. It was the first time in a long while the department had been addressed directly. Since Lenny never bothered remembering Alfonzo's name, he'd written,

Dear Mr. Camellama,

I am reaching out in regards to the implementation of the mayor's multiphase project to update infrastructure within City Hall.

In my position as Director of Operations for the mayor, I am tasked with identifying and removing any hindrance to the implementation of this plan.

Old Spots liked his verbiage ominous. Alfonzo coughed up an underdigested grass ball. He tasted nervous bile.

After extensive study it has been determined that the current tube system of communication used in the Hall may be allowing water to leak into the basement. Mould is a pressing concern. To that end,

Seadyne Industries has been contracted to clean and seal City Hall's tube system. This will be phase one of a bold project to replace all decaying tubing with a state-of-the-art system made with customized patented mould-resistant Beewell Industries Horse Whisperer™ tubing.

Mould was obviously a problem, but this was the first time Alfonzo was hearing that anyone upstairs cared about the sorry state of the underbuilding. Perhaps he would get time off with pay? Alfonzo skimmed the rest of the letter.

Because of the danger to the health of employees such as yourself, it will be necessary to close the basement starting tomorrow (Friday). Please enjoy this extra day off. On Monday morning, specialists from Seadyne will be on-site to begin the process of relocating files to their facilities and retiring obsolete machinery. In consultation with their specialists and the office of the mayor, I will be reviewing the future staffing needs for the department, if indeed there are any. To that end, I would like to meet next Monday morning at 10:30 a.m. to discuss your position at City Hall going forward.

Alfonzo peered around the dark cavern in disbelief. He was getting fired. Maybe. *Was this or was this not his den?* It was true that sometimes he'd wished to leave. Over the years, he'd fantasized about moving from this basement. But he'd thought that if they were to part ways it would be his choice. He'd joked about getting fired to Mitchell too many times to count, probably because neither of them considered it a real possibility. His options began to spin like newspapers in a black-and-white headline montage.

ALPACA WORKER ABRUPTLY SACKED, BUT HE
    VOWS A FIGHT
SPRING CLEANING IN THE ARCHIVES: GOOD
    RIDDANCE TO BAD RUBBISH
THE ENDANGERED PUBLIC SERVANT: ONE
    ANIMAL'S TAIL

He'd have to call his union, but he wondered what could be done beyond securing some severance. If they found a way to fire him for cause, he probably wouldn't get even that. If they dug (and what pig wasn't good at smelling out dirt?), they'd probably be able to find evidence of all the paper he'd pilfered over the seasons. The dissertation was only the latest time he'd misappropriated office supplies. He had about a hundred City Hall pens at home. He had a whole drawer full of sticky-note pads. Sure, it felt small, but theft could be theft if they wanted him gone. Maybe the fact they'd messed up his name could be used as protection. Was that how plausible deniability worked?

He had taken this protective space for granted, the protection the archive offered, and now he was being ejected, just as the old Howtek printer was being "retired." Probably that meant they'd chuck the machine into Fresh Kills along with all the other pieces of elder machinery.

He was sure that once Old Spots and Seadyne got involved, he'd never again see the inside of this office. You can't bite City Hall, only struggle while they push you out under the guise of cleaning up mould. He should have known. He'd have to tell his father he was out of work, and sharing this would be infinitely worse than the dissertation admission. He'd have to move back into his childhood bedroom and live with Luis. He'd become one of those teetering old animals bickering with their even more ancient parent up and down the aisles of Super Foodtown.

Alfonzo needed Mitchell's help, yet again. He scribbled a note, then taped it to the archive door: OUT OF OFFICE, BACK IN 10.

19.

Alfonzo peered around the corner, surveying the upstairs hallway landscape for predatory pigs. He knew the city council was in session, so most animals were occupied, but still he didn't want to attract attention. As he tried to sneak soundlessly to Mitchell's office, Alfonzo arranged his features into a neutral expression. *Act natural*, he told himself. *Project a relaxed and yet professional vibe.* His wool was springy with sweat.

He made it undetected but found that the glossy white door with a frosted pane and gold lettering that spelled out DEPARTMENT OF AFFORDABLE HOUSING was shut. Taped to the front was a sign written in familiar chicken scratch: BACK SOON!

All right, all right, all right. Alfonzo would go get a coffee, real casual. He would likely find Mitchell at his favourite haunt, the Early Cenozoic.

"You looking for that deadbeat, too?"

Alfonzo leapt up in fright, almost kicking Lenny Old Spots on his way down.

"A little high-strung, hey, fella?"

"Sorry, Lenny. I just, well, you never know who's going to lunge out and grab your neck in their jaws.

Predators lurking around every corner. If you know what I mean. I mean, sorry, that's insensitive."

"I get it. Some herbivores are all nerves. I've personally never let those reflexes get out of control, but I do know how it is. I have a sister who can't look at an itty-bitty fox without having a heart attack, and she's two hundred pounds."

The pig snuffled. The alpaca twitched. They faced each other, swaying slightly. Alfonzo bent his head in a sign of submission. He hoped that would get the pig to leave. Old Spots stayed put.

"Say. Sorry about this—it's my memory going—but I might have written your name wrong on a memo I sent?"

Alfonzo cycled through the possibilities. Old Spots was fucking with him, playing some seven-dimensional porcine chess. Or the pig sincerely didn't know Alfonzo's name. But Old Spots knew he was the one in the basement. He didn't want to get wrapped up in too much conversation, in case the pig tried to use Alfonzo's words against him.

"I . . ." Alfonzo snuffled. "I mean, you can call me Al."

"Well, Al, I don't envy you down there with all those tubes and soggy paper. Shitty job."

"Ah, yes, well, someone's got to do it."

"Donkey's work."

"Hum?"

"It goes on and on forever. You haven't heard that?"

"No, sir."

"You don't know the saying 'Donkeys live a long time'?"

"Longer than other folks?"

"Have you ever seen a dead donkey?"

"Ah. *Hum.* Good one, sir."

The pig harrumphed. "Not really a joke, son. I've known some donkeys. Lemme tell you, the saying comes from somewhere. They're like lobsters, they don't die. Anyhow, I wouldn't waste much time on your friend. That camel spends more time out of the office than in. I need to check on some papers, but he's never where I want him. Actually, since you're a document fellow, maybe you could help."

"Camelids." Alfonzo felt feverish.

"What?"

"Not to be oversensitive, but we're not—"

"Oh, right. Not a camel. So sensitive. I'm sorry you were offended."

"No prob-llama." Alfonzo hoped a pun would drive the pig away, but Old Spots just smirked.

"Anyhow, we'll find what we need when the Seadyne boys come in. They know how to get things going. They should be an inspiration to the likes of you."

"Hum?"

"Two words: Private. Sector. Look for a job where they really move that paper," Old Spots stage-whispered, then nipped Alfonzo's knee.

Alfonzo jerked.

"But, I mean, you didn't hear that from me, right?"

"Who, me? No! I don't hear anything but the pipes whistling."

"Whistling while they work, am I right, chief? Okay.

You know nothing. Nothing is good to hear. You'll be hearing about next steps soon enough."

And with that, Old Spots turned on his hooves and clicked away down the hall. Alfonzo's stomachs wrapped themselves around his spine. He felt faint. He chewed hard on his wad of breakfast grass in an effort to rein in his nerves.

He caught a subtle movement. It was Mitchell's door inching open. A familiar eye peered through the crack.

"Shush."

"What are you doing, you loon?" Alfonzo hummed. They were all going crazy.

Mitchell eased open his door just wide enough to yank his friend into his office.

Mitchell hovered with ears pricked in case Old Spots decided to return. When he finally relaxed, he indicated with his wrinkled brow that they should use the lowest possible tones. They both wagged their tails nervously.

"Where have you been?" Mitchell whispered. "I've sent you three emergency tube messages."

Ah, yes, Alfonzo realized, this plan of the mayor's must be much bigger than he imagined.

"Did you get a memo, too? About Seadyne? I got a memo! Or, rather, the department did. I think they're trying to shrink Records to nothing. What does this mean? Have you heard?"

Mitchell waggled his ears yes and then no. He gave a few exaggerated winks. What he said next he didn't even say, but rather mouthed the words. Knot. Ear. Fat. The. Hen. Oh woe. Ticks.

But who was Fat the Hen? It didn't make sense. Alfonzo was a terrible lip reader.

"We need to go on another site visit."

Alfonzo was annoyed. "Now isn't the time for sneaking out to the shore."

Even though they'd seen each other, Mitchell and he hadn't really been talking. Alfonzo had been tangled in his sadness. A gap had opened that misunderstanding crept into. Alfonzo tried once again to get an answer. What should he do to prevent being downsized or investigated or booted because of misuse of office resources, broken tubes, and basement leaks?

"Did you get a memo this morning or was it just me?"

"No." Mitchell nodded yes.

Alfonzo was going to lose his job, and his main ally was behaving like a harebrained secret agent. This goofy caterpillar-looking ass llama was going to ruin his life. Mitchell leaned over and bit Alfonzo. Not hard, but still. Physical violence always took him by surprise. Again with the biting.

"Alfonzo. Come. With. Me."

He did as his friend asked.

"Mitchell?"

"Hum?"

"What's happening?"

"I told you, not here. At the Cenozoic."

"You didn't."

"I did."

"Mitchell, what's happening in City Hall?"

"A little bird told me something big," Mitchell hummed.

"Is that Fat the Hen? Sounds like not a little bird, but does she know if they're shutting down my department? The place that pays me money to live on? Are ticks and mould related?" Alfonzo lowered his voice. "Is this some kind of Deep Throat situation? Is Fiona from the Parks Department Fat the Hen? She seems so guileless."

"There is no hen! *A little bird told me* is a figure of speech. I know things, but it will take some time to lay it all out."

"Like a chicken lays eggs?"

"Shut up."

Alfonzo had to get it out in the open. He felt so guilty. "I think Old Spots is going to fire me because of the printing."

"What?"

"I think Old Spots will look for mould and find stolen paper."

"Why do you think that?"

"It just follows. I think I may have implicated you in my paper theft, and now that pig is trying to psych me out by calling me 'Mr. Camellama.'"

"Oh," Mitchell sighed. "You poor hysterical creature. I'm the one who should be sorry. The mayor isn't trying to get you—he doesn't know you exist—and Old Spots is just a toady. What they're after are the files I gave you."

Mitchell pushed the door open. A bell rang, and Mitchell let out a little whistle. They entered the Early Cenozoic.

20.

E.M.U. was playing on the stereo. The song reminded Alfonzo of college. He had a ripple of a memory of Vivi, their meeting. He recalled walking down a stairway into a den. He remembered a ratty orange couch and a stereo blasting. He asked Vivi something stupid and she ended up telling him about a dance essay she was writing on the Eight Efforts: to float, to thrust, to glide, to slash, to dab, to wring, to flick, and to press. These were building blocks of motion. She told him the story of her childhood ship voyage from Lima to New York. They'd smoked catnip, and Mitchell had hummed everything he knew about E.M.U., which was probably too much. He'd always had the ability to retain minutiae about bands and musicians he loved.

The Early Cenozoic was in a lull between morning and the lunch rush. Pamella the barista was tending some suspended air plants. The decor had changed since Alfonzo's last visit. The wallpaper behind the plants was a new pattern of cosmic splatter swirls against a blue-purple background. The walls pulsed like a display at the natural history museum. Environments can change so easily—you look away for a moment, and leaves burst from trees, paint transforms an interior. Look away again and when your eyes return, those leaves have browned and fallen and there's a FOR RENT sign in the window of the freshly painted room. Over a weekend, a café can go from white cube to stars and moon. A vibration you've only just managed to feel can disappear before you have a chance to locate its source.

Mitchell called out to Pamella, "Can you chat with us for a moment?"

"If you buy something."

"Two salad boxes." Mitchell turned to Alfonzo. "One thing I haven't told you, but probably should, is that Pamella and I have been seeing each other."

Pamella brought the greens.

"Have I formally introduced you?" Mitchell asked. "This is my friend for life, and this is my sister in the struggle."

"Hey," Alfonzo said.

"Hey."

"Hay is for horses," Mitchell added.

"Oh my, you two, always with the jokes."

"So, Pamella, I think this will be of interest: Alfonzo is scared because Shergar has made a move. They're closing the basement and bringing in Seadyne to rehab the pipes, and fix 'leaks.' He's worried they're going to discover his paper trail."

Her round eyes became bigger and rounder. "Interesting," the lemur chirped.

"This is the moment I have to tell our dear alpaca everything."

Pamella reached out her paw and squeezed Alfonzo's shoulder in a sisterly way. She said, "Go with the flow."

Alfonzo studied the wooden benches, the potted plants, the big glass window framing a building being renovated. Half the building was its old self, a reddish brick affair, and half was a future self of glass and exposed metal beams. A yellow crane arched its huge neck over the building's exposed guts.

Mitchell began humming in such a strange way that Alfonzo could do nothing but listen.

"I knew the bubble was going to burst; I just didn't know what would do it. This is a kind of relief because it forces us to act rather than continue to wait and watch. I did hope it would take longer, as I am only beginning, only now meeting the animals, only now learning to breathe in a new way. But one cannot pick the battles of one's era.

"Something started to change when I began doing site visits," Mitchell continued. "I had a sense of satisfaction and variation in my work, for once. I would knock on doors, hear stories, help these animals navigate the necessary bureaucracy and sometimes their living situations would improve. I believed that we were there to help. It wasn't easy, but I was satisfied that I was able to play a small part in the recovery. But then, as time passed, I kept hearing these stories . . . I got messages about flooded basements and broken water mains, evictions and homelessness. At first, it felt random, or explainable by way of 'natural' disaster and aging infrastructure. For a while, I just kept my head down and stewed. I kept working to move animals through the gauntlet of city housing. But I began to realize that all these overlapping stories were not one-offs, but patterned. The pattern took the form of corporate takeovers and sell-offs, expulsions and redevelopments." Mitchell dropped to his quietest hum. "I have been collecting evidence of what we believe is a large-scale conspiracy by the mayor to give Seadyne huge deals to renovate public housing."

"Is that illegal? They're constantly writing in the papers that Seadyne and the city are partners."

"Well, what they're not announcing is that over the course of those 'renovations' Seadyne finds—actually, it creates—structural problems by drilling holes, opening up cracks, and, most insidiously, flooding basements. Much of the damage comes from water they pump into basements. This plan, as far as we know, was devised in the aftermath of Hurricane Sparky. They found that the sea was a perfect scapegoat. Mention a flood, and everyone goes wild.

"So Seadyne workers wreck a building, and then they deliver reports to the mayor that say the buildings are rotten, uninhabitable, and too expensive to save. The mayor then advocates selling the buildings and relocating residents. This shuffles the problem to the future, and in the meantime the mayor is richer and the residents are rendered homeless. Both Seadyne and Shergar avoid taxes, and scrutiny. Shergar's wealth increases, and Seadyne gobbles up once publicly owned land for discount rates.

"Remember after the hurricane, there was so much grief. Birds crying over broken eggs. Cats stuck in trees for days, bedraggled from rain and half starved. Injured donkeys dragging themselves out of collapsed sheds. There were so many calls for unity and compassion. But what I realized as I researched is that Mayor Shergar and his associates—the many tentacles of the power class— did not want to help. They *want* things to go as badly as possible. Suffering is at the root of these fortunes."

It hurt Alfonzo that Mitchell hadn't told him sooner. Mitchell scoffed.

"I would have helped," Alfonzo offered.

"You've been so wrapped up. I tried to show you. I've been introducing you to my contacts, to the whole network. I thought if I did it slowly, you'd take it better. But you couldn't see past your despair . . ."

"Who is the network? Those cats from the shore? Wait . . ." Alfonzo's stomachs clenched with the memory of the small blue book he'd read and then forgotten. "Are you . . ." He struggled for the term. "A SERF? Is that what they're even called? Aren't they dangerous?"

"I didn't want to tell you until everything was ready. But the timeline has changed. And they are not dangerous—it's the land creatures who are," Mitchell hummed.

Mitchell then began a new hum. It was a strange hum, filled with rage and joy. It was not loud, but it enveloped Alfonzo's whole body, from ears to tail. He felt safe for the first time in a while, as if all the pressure and pain of the past seasons were dissolved by the hum.

"SERFs are all around. I am SERF. Pamella is SERF. Lipstick and Tuxedo are SERF. Akida Kombu is SERF.

And I will tell you something more, something I know will touch your heart: Viviana is SERF. SERF has been all around you in secret. And you, my friend, you are becoming SERF as well. Without knowing it, you have already contributed greatly to the SERF cause."

"How?" Alfonzo could only croak.

"That paper I gave for your dissertation wasn't recycling. It's the evidence of dealings between the mayor and Seadyne. On the back sides of your dissertation are financial files. It was how I smuggled the truth out of City Hall. I am a leak, and so are you."

21.

The llama and the alpaca hunched side by side on Alfonzo's apartment floor, with their long necks arched over scattered dissertation pages. Alfonzo wanted to see the evidence with his own eyes. Cigarette and catnip clouded the room.

"The mice neighbours are probably furious with me," Alfonzo said.

"Maybe they consider second-hand smoke a bonus. Free cigarettes!" Mitchell lit another. "Do you talk to them?" he asked.

"I think my size makes them nervous."

"It might be that they know too much about you, your comings and goings, your musical tastes and your phone calls."

"They've heard me cry, that's for sure."

Alfonzo studied the papers. They revealed that Appleby, Dowd, and Associates had arranged shell companies for the mayor and Seadyne. Seadyne paid Seahorse Co. $13.8 million for concrete that was never delivered. Seadyne paid Cheyne Enterprises $65.6 million in consulting fees. Behind Seahorse and Cheyne and Amsea were members of the mayor's family. Cheyne Enterprises, for one, was registered as a company in the fiscal paradise of Bermuda in the name of Shergar's adolescent daughter, Cinnamon.

"It must be hard to work as a building consultant while still in junior high."

"Earning $65.5 million while also playing junior varsity polo is quite a feat."

"Are you implying rich kids aren't hard-working enough to do it all?"

"I'd never dare."

Alfonzo wondered if he would have understood the implications if his best friend hadn't been beside him as a guide. Who calls a bribe a bribe? How do you know a bribe isn't a donation? What's the difference between a payment and a payoff? It was rarely a matter of unmarked bills in briefcases. So many things look similar in the backwaters of Paperwork River, and that river flows into oceans of debt. City money finds itself offshore in the Caymans and the Seychelles. It boggled Alfonzo, though he should have known.

"Weren't they rich already?" he asked.

"It's never enough," Mitchell ruminated. "The rich, who thieve to live, then go ahead and play a trick, a thousand tricks, that serve to rename their stealing 'job creation' and 'CEO compensation.' They call it 'competitiveness,' and they call it 'natural.' The law of nature. Eat or be eaten. If you want more, work harder. Respect the hustle. And what's staggering is that we accept those words and parrot them back. They've trapped everyone in the conceptual net, so threats to capital are felt by every homeowner and pensioner."

Mitchell was really getting going. "Not everyone believes, of course. But still, the net is there. Obedience-school loans, credit card debt, underwater cat condos. Not believing in it doesn't win you an exemption. Debt holds even non-believers down. There's always jail. The urge to stockpile wealth is a symptom of the disease, but it's also the illness itself. The rich are sick, and if money were anything else, we'd see their hoarding for what it was. Nothing for them will ever be enough. Riches are rabies."

Alfonzo sniffed. The sheets before him were blurred and smudgy. The problem was that, at this level, greed was nothing but a number. There was no visible blood, no death. *We have to go on talking together*, he thought, *reminding one another about the ideology of violence and theft that lies beneath the numbers. We have to care and work as a whole herd to make it matter.*

"Tell me the plan."

Mitchell twisted uncertainly. "I have to believe that animals will do something when faced with proof they're being robbed by those they elected to serve."

When his uncle Ernie had first gotten him his job, Mitchell was just out of college with a dual degree in zoology and political science. He'd changed his major too many times, from history to prelaw to wildlands management to landscape architecture. He talked his dad's ears off about a class on wetlands. Mitchell then wondered if perhaps journalism or radio might suit him, but he thought his voice sounded funny recorded, so he switched to animal psychology. He loved to think about how everyone thought. He took a class on modern government, which led to a political science minor. His advisers threw up their paws. "Just make up your mind and stick with it," they said. School was like playing musical chairs against himself. He liked the circling and the songs, but as the semesters kept coming and going, the seating options diminished. In the end he had his butt in only two places, and that felt like some kind of victory.

His consciousness was scattered, unformed, and disobedient. He used to believe without real proof that the system worked. Anyway, the government seemed to work well enough. Mitchell followed his uncle's advice when it came to work and spent most of his time outside the office thinking about friendship and romance. But through the experience, his sense of injustice intensified, and through romance that sense found a language.

Mitchell's work took him through kitchens and dens, onto fire escapes, and into the utility rooms of the five boroughs. He heard stories of pit bulls with sledgehammers patrolling a building's halls in an effort to scare tenants out of a rent-controlled apartment. Animals left without running water or working toilets. He saw with his own eyes black mould and hanging wires and stairs without railings. He saw building after building with signs that read PLEASE CONTACT SEADYNE INC. FOR INFORMATION ON ONGOING RENOVATIONS. He wrote report after report that vanished into the pneumatic tubes, never to receive a comment or a work order. Mitchell got frustrated. How do you fight City Hall from within its many-organed body?

Was it love at first sight with Pamella? Mitchell had never been a romantic in that way, but there was a flash, a coup de foudre. Soon after they met at the Early Cenozoic, he told her she was beautiful and that he wanted to protect her from all predators.

She shook her head at that offer.

Through Pamella, Mitchell had met a network of creatures who still had hope. They went beyond identifying the negative; they talked of alternatives. He'd met the cats Lipstick and Tuxedo. These new secret friends gave him things to read: F-SERF dispatches, midnight notes, poems. They said, as if it were simple, that housing was a basic right, that lands should be common, that the sea was family. When Mitchell asked what he could do, they hatched the plan for Mitchell to squirrel away bits of evidence of the mayor's transgressions.

Alfonzo asked, "Have you joined a revolutionary organization?"

"It's not like there's a membership card or anything."

"Why did you keep all this from me?"

"I was waiting for the right time."

Mitchell didn't think anyone in the mayor's office knew what he knew, though Old Spots was always fishing.

"What will you do with the documents?"

"Give them to the press," Mitchell declared.

Alfonzo felt like a frayed knot, a weak link. He didn't want to let Mitchell down, yet he couldn't help but imagine from an outside perspective. He imagined his father reading the paper. What if they—Mitchell and Pamella, or Lipstick and Tuxedo, or SERF, or whoever—

proved the mayor was a criminal dung stain robbing the city blind? So what? The best-case scenario was Shergar resigning and another billionaire or billionaire's lackey getting put in his place. More probable was that the story of a housing crisis and a rich mayor's offshore money would become just another opportunity for equivocation and the murk of conspiracy.

"Consider the news, Mitchell. Just think about how you'll get portrayed. A mid-level bureaucrat meets some dirtbags and an immigrant radical. They recruit him into a secret ocean-animal liberation movement—which, by the by, many animals, including our very powerful mayor, calls a terrorist organization. Inspired by these ne'er-do-wells, he begins investigating the mayor while on company time and, justified by anti-capitalist theory, starts stealing official documents. In the process, he unilaterally decides to implicate his childhood friend in this scheme, thereby setting not only his own life on the path to ruin but also that of his dumb friend. Just imagine that splashed across the *Post*. Think of the headlines!"

"Many land animals do secretly trust the sea," Mitchell insisted. "The sea is our mother."

"So your plan is to send my dissertation to reporters?" Alfonzo asked.

"Oh, don't worry, they won't read it. It's just the back of the real important stuff."

"I'll be both exposed and reminded that my life's work is irrelevant. Cool, cool, cool."

Mitchell huffed, "I used your work as a means, it's true. But it was for something important. SERF wants to topple the mayor so that we can communicate again, sea and land. If animals knew, maybe they would rise."

"Like the tides?"

Humming and silence, silence and humming. It wasn't that Alfonzo didn't agree with Mitchell, it was just that he was afraid for them.

It wasn't that Alfonzo didn't want liberation. He just despaired of its possibility.

22.

There's always something below. There's a sole beneath toes, soil under the sole, stones supporting the soil, bugs hiding between the stones, tongues searching for the bugs, and a stomach to digest them once the hunting tongue gets ahold. Stairs lead to basements that lead to doors to sub-basements. Under the subway lies the sewer. Beneath the street, power and water, cable and steam pipes spaghetti through compromised earth. Every tree twists its roots down and around the archaeological remnants from older versions of the city. Roots seek water while water finds its level, regardless of the rock and concrete that tries to block its flow.

A canal lies buried beneath Canal Street. Freshwater streams meander under luxury brownstones of the Upper West Side. Bedrock only occasionally shows itself in Central Park, like the nose of a mole or the top of an iceberg. To know one doesn't know is the foundation of knowledge.

Just the same, there is always something above, a tree branch, an overpass, a storm pregnant with rain, the ozone layer's fragile mist. There is always more. We animals are held exquisitely between.

Alfonzo envisioned himself on a path wrapped along a mountain. To his left rose a cliff face. On the other side was space, and a long fall to the crashing sea. He didn't know where the narrow path led, but there was no room to turn.

There was a story about his species. It was said that when the European animals came to South America to plun-der, they forced llamas and alpacas into servitude. They made them carry gold and silver down from the moun-tains to waiting ships. Llamas, though anguished, bore their sacks. Alpacas, however, refused. No matter how much they were beaten and kicked by the invaders, the alpacas resisted, even to the death. They would rather be cut into a thousand pieces than move against their will.

What was his choice? What could he choose? Follow the path where it leads, freeze in place, or fall. If he must go toward the unknown, Alfonzo thought, it would be his choice. He wasn't about to be pulled or pushed. He would walk himself.

That night, Alfonzo gave Mitchell his blessing and his dissertation. He said he needed to be alone to digest.

"Take all the time you need," Mitchell said. "When you are ready, go to the café. Pamella will know what to do."

Alfonzo promised. They both squirmed a bit with feeling.

"I want you to know that you are my brother." Two big tears fell from Mitchell's eyes.

"No matter what," Alfonzo hummed.

"You're a good boy."

"Ha."

"See you?"

"Sea you soon."

Alone, Alfonzo smoked a cigarette for courage, and when there was nothing else to do, he hummed a prayer and dialled the number for Viviana Lopez-Cuña.

BENEATH THE BEACH

23.

Viviana Lopez-Cuña came from a family of graceful shadows. They flickered even, or perhaps especially, in front of one another. The breeze of sadness never ceased.

In their youth, her parents, Nancy—called Naya by friends—and Adriano, had helped found a dissident art movement called Zanistoism. It was really just a loose affiliation of artists and intellectuals who'd attended the Zana University of Science and Arts in Peru, but Adriano had penned a manifesto with his friends and the art world had latched on. A manifesto does a tidy job of defining the limits of an *ism*, which later scholars appreciate.

Vivi's parents' names appeared passingly in art books she read in college. She could never find pictures of them, though. It was only their friends and enemies who appeared in the photos, animals she'd heard abstract gossip about while she was growing up, animals who were now either old or dead. In the pictures, they appeared as young animals leaping around doing dances before brightly painted abstract cloths strung up in fields, or gathered in a dingy warehouse practising plays. Her parents were considered minor, background figures in their country's art world. But that was still something. All the creatures in the photos looked so confident in their beauty and their good ideas.

A long time before Vivi existed, when Adriano and Naya were still renegade Andean artists painting rivers and staging plays about atheism and free sea love, Naya gave birth to Vivi's brother, Silvio. Silvio was her parents' darling baby when they themselves were just students. The three of them grew up together. All the wild fun seemed to have been had before her birth. By the time Vivi was aware, her parents and her brother were grown and serious. Her parents had teaching jobs; they debated politics, drank coffees, and shared the secrets of adulthood with Silvio. In retrospect, Vivi knew that Silvio was still an adolescent in those years, still a high school student, but Vivi always knew him as her parents' beloved peer. They poured him small glasses of their wine and let him smoke on the balcony. They debated enclosures and grain riots and bird separatism while Vivi drank her milk and played with bits of string on the floor. Her father never condescended to Silvio the way he did to Vivi. She was the little girl who tripped over her own toes. Silvio was the genius son who excelled at chess and astronomy and won awards at school.

Silvio's death was Vivi's hinge. Before and after pivoted on that event.

One night when Silvio was in college, he went out and never came back. Her parents thought perhaps he had a secret love. The next day Vivi went to school and dance class as usual. When the second night passed, the anxiety overwhelmed her parents. They called Silvio's friends. The next morning they visited the university and then the hospitals. They reluctantly got the police involved. She overheard her folks murmuring about car accidents, comas, predators, drowning in a well. They made Vivi keep going to school, though she cried to stay. When she returned, the apartment was filled with the whole herd, every vicuña in Zana, and every member of the Zanistos, too, no matter the species, crowding, smoking, and fretting. Each time the door would open, all heads would turn in concert, a flight of stares. The phone kept ringing, but the caller never had news of Silvio.

Like all vicuñas, Vivi and her family were skinny, large-eyed, and high-strung. Her father sometimes wore three shirts to make himself more formidable on the street, but the real effect was slightly absurdist. The family shared the same fine white-and-cinnamon coat. Ever after Silvio's disappearance, her parents agonized over the possibility that he could have been killed for his wool. Shambling along a dark Zana alley, humming a chamber piece to himself, Silvio would have been an ideal target for those who looked at vicuñas and saw only profit.

The police never found anything, though no one expected that corrupt den of wolves to help. The university was plastered with posters of Silvio's face for weeks.

Some months later, a friend of her parents', one of the most prominent Zanistos, an artist-theorist bear in spectacles who had gotten a plum professorship in Upstate New York, wangled a fellowship for Vivi's father.

Her parents never wanted to move to America. They would have stayed in Zana forever, waiting for their son to return. Their friends had to drag them to the bus station.

After a fourteen-hour bus ride during which her mother only cried and slept, they boarded a ship bound for New York through the Panama Canal. Vivi never again saw Peru. Silvio became a phantom from her lost world.

Her parents managed their grief by dedicating all their new work to their disappeared son. Naya typed out a book about Silvio, about missing sons and daughters, that Adriano had written on yellow legal pads. The absence came to define her parents' minds. Though they never knew the circumstances of Silvio's disappearance, their imaginings soon went beyond their original notions of robbery gone wrong or wool-murder. Maybe it was a political punishment; maybe he'd spoken up at school about the president. They linked Silvio to their own dissident art. Her parents' pain made them even more eloquent than they had been before. After writing his second book—the famous one on animal rights and creative resistance—her father was invited to speak at other universities and art institutes.

Vivi was very withdrawn during high school. Her New York classmates voted her Most Ghostlike, and she joked to herself about the stupidity of voting anybody anything. She found her new country shrill. It deafened her. She tiptoed through her house and listened to phone calls through doors. She lost herself in dancing because it didn't require speech. The first thing she appreciated about Alfonzo was his habit of leaning in and speaking softly. She had chosen Hapshire College because it was surrounded by majestic trees that muffled sounds. Vivi swaddled her body in layers: scarves and leg warmers and army surplus jackets. She threw herself into dance and psychology classes, and only saw Adriano and Naya at holidays. Only a few friends ever heard the story of Silvio. One, naturally, was Alfonzo, her first, truest love.

24.

Sometimes the vicuña whom an alpaca loved but rejected out of grief is not so lost. This era has so many air pockets. Extinct love might not be extinct. We can change our relationships. Sometimes the vicuña whom an alpaca loved but rejected is living only a few hours away, taking care of a rich dog's beach house. Sometimes the alpaca can put aside his pride and shame and call the vicuña to talk about sea revolutions, and family wounds, and fights against corrupt mayors. It can even happen that the vicuña understands it all and invites the alpaca to visit. Trains to the shore leave every few hours from Atlantic Station. Animals smell one another's emotional states. Many things are possible.

Viviana was living temporarily at the End of the World, a small island enclave off Long Island's tip. To get there, Alfonzo would take the Ronkonkoma line to the last stop and then catch a ferry. She told him to meet her at the Red Clover Tavern.

He slept late and deep. He woke with a start, gulped a coffee, and did some version of packing by shoving a bottle of seltzer, a bag of kale chips, and a music magazine into a sack. He wound himself in a scarf, then set off toward the station. Afternoon sun beamed through half clouds, refracting billions of water droplets. This was no usual Friday afternoon. He felt giddy and wild. If this was what it could be like, he would take the layoff. A cold wind blew. He rushed down the sidewalk in an attempt to stay warm. He should have brought a coat. Stay calm. *Act natural*, he hummed.

Exhaustion and hurry gave the station a frantic odour. A group of birds shared fries on a bench, squawking at passing cats. A deranged goose and a maintenance possum hissed at each other. He trod carefully to avoid tails and feet.

He made a transfer at Jamaica Station. On the next train there were a few creatures. He eavesdropped on older trade union beavers, but then they got off at Yaphank, leaving him without distraction.

Once the train was clear of the city's force field, suburban colours flickered by the windows. A red house sheltered beneath a tree of yellow leaves. He'd forgotten how grand trees could be. Then the train sped up, and the streets, yards, big-box stores, and flora smeared. The train paused at Deer Park.

Alfonzo drifted off, then woke with drool in his wool. Outside were boats in backyards, hints of the sea's proximity bathed in pools of artificial light. He ate the whole bag of kale chips while staring into the dark. This was adolescent. He should have had a real dinner like a grown alpaca.

In the train bathroom he studied himself, tried to see himself as Vivi would. Older and chubbier. Lips still curled in persistent bemusement. He couldn't help his cartoon softness, round nostrils, big eyes, the smattering of white mixed in with his brown curls in need of a trim. He saw the animal he was. What would it be like to look and be looked at by the one he loved but was no longer with?

When he returned to his seat, dark had fully fallen outside, so he took up his magazine. It was an issue of *Slug and Lettuce* containing a long interview with Akida Kombu. Now he realized it was a secret SERF message. It was revolutionary material in disguise by being totally undisguised.

DEEP ADAPTATION: AN INTERVIEW WITH SONIC LEGEND AKIDA KOMBU

"Viva, Comrade Animal, viva! . . . Long live the fresh air, long live! . . . Forward with the struggle for the purification and preservation of all the elements of nature, forward!"
—Piwe Mkhize, from "Back to Nature," in *Literature of Nature: An International Sourcebook*

There was a photo of the musician, serious and fluffy, standing on the beach surrounded by homemade instruments. Ink-green seaweed twisted behind in this portrait of an artist as an eccentric sea dog. Kombu's outlook was dark, mystical, and charged with discordant romance. He was famed for playing both above and below the surface of the sea.

The interviewer asked: *How did you come to music?*

"I was first influenced by aggressive sounds. I grew up close to a shipyard; many hours of rock and roll came from the radio where dock animals worked. It was always a mix of the Stones and waves. The ships brought goods in and out, and they did the same with music, musical cargo. I heard gazelle Dabke, Thai country, birdsong from Agadez, jungle slowcore, Sufi snake rock, and whale songs just by hanging around the port.

"I was also friends with many seals and seabirds. They were outcasts who knew the level of violence the land could unleash, but they also loved music from everywhere. We listened to the pulsations of radio pop as it distorted over the water. These friends were artists who first opened my ears to whole new levels of sound. These listening experiences alerted me to levels my rational mind could not perceive.

"But since the sea does not have the musical industry that land does, I only realized it was possible to be a musician professionally by looking around on land. I first tried playing drums with some land band, but that could not satisfy me, so I broke out on my own."

Everyone would agree that your music is shattering, especially in terms of volume. Could you expand on your commitment to intense noise?

"I came to noise through a process of discovery. What could my body withstand, what could other bodies withstand? Could we find a still point in a storm? Almost technical. I wanted to reproduce street noise, machine noise, construction noise, but also trench noise, wave noise, and mesopelagic noise, all at once. What I make becomes a space to meditate inside. A lost sphere or temporary autonomous zone.

"For the sea-bound, sounding is like breathing. The whole body is—and is in—sound. From the sea I learned that shattering sound could heal and that the whole body was sounding all the time. So, although those on land think I am always loud, those in the sea also know I have a whole level you would call silent. I think intense noise has become my way of communicating the plight of the seas to those on land. In that way, loud noise is more political, I suppose."

Political in what way?

"You see, I have made my life with many seals. They taught me to swim, to be at peace in the water. I think they are my community, and I want to transmit their feelings or what I understand of their feelings into something those on land can comprehend. I can be both in sea and on land. One webbed paw in each realm. And the violence between them is unbearable. But really it is not between, it is one-sided. There is violence perpetrated by land against the sea. There are kinds of violence that flow through every part of the sea and yet remain almost invisible to those on land. There is the chronic noise of ships, propellers grinding, huge explosions of low frequency that create a bed on which we are forced to lie. This has been the case for generations, as the land has industrialized.

"But companies also use air guns to search for fossil

fuels. They are six or seven times louder than ship sounds. Many companies are using these non-stop, every ten seconds, for months at a time. It starts as a big bang and changes to a reverberating fuzz. I think many on land imagine the ocean as a quiet place. Those in the sea are living through endless, shattering storms. So, what I try to do is return the noise land companies are imposing onto the sea back to those on land. This is my form of resistance."

Do you need for your audience to get these ideas to understand your music?

"I have written many things about the sea struggle. I think that the curious will educate themselves. To communicate, one must take the indirect route."

The train arrived. Alfonzo made his way to the ferry. Above was a cold, humid tarp of pearl-coloured clouds and black sky. Sea and sky shone against each other in reflection. There were stars where there weren't clouds.

The boat moved over the spangled sea through soft air. Was he inside or outside the bubble? Was this outer space? The delicacy overwhelmed him. The dense air was so fresh, Alfonzo needed a cigarette to breathe more normally. He bummed a smoke from an older sheep and puffed it into the dark.

They floated past a series of wooden posts sticking up above the water. A group of birds gathered, one perched on each post. The birds wore hats and were also smoking. Their little orange ember tips glowed. This was how shore birds relaxed together, he thought. All the animals of the world are so close, and yet we can be so ignorant. He thought of all the birds he'd crossed paths with. How little he knew of their aerial views, their feathers, and struggles. *We are one another's aliens*, he thought.

25.

Vivi was at the Red Clover Tavern as promised, sitting beside an elephant named Krithi Devi. Krithi was from Kerala, India, but she was living in exile because her activism for other females had brought her death threats. Afraid for her elderly parents, she'd succumbed to pressure and gone abroad. She'd ended up stuck in Long Island, at the End of the World, because the boat she'd been travelling on had sprung a leak. She and her travelling companions were hanging around this off-season beach town, waiting for some parts to arrive by mail so the ship could be repaired. She and Vivi hit it off because they could sit with each other, talking sometimes but also letting silences exist. The elephant was accompanied everywhere by a yellow-and-red-beaked bird named Edith. Edith never drank or chatted; all she did was glare intently at anyone who came near Krithi. No one felt comfortable asking about the bird's behaviour.

That night the bar was full, perhaps because of the band. Vivi was anxious and ended up explaining her history with Alfonzo to her friend, who only wobbled her head sympathetically. All the while, Edith pecked delicately at Krithi's ear.

Alfonzo arrived. He picked Vivi out from the crowd right away. He was surprised by the atmosphere. There were a few cats and dogs, a couple of beavers, a deer chatting with a turkey, and an osprey in a baseball hat sitting alone with a newspaper and a beer. There was also the elephant beside Vivi. As he made his way through the long room, he passed a circle of seals and sea lions curled around a table in one of the dim recesses. Alfonzo didn't stare, but he did steal a few glances. The sea creatures were so large and sleek. They almost disappeared into the dark, but then the light would catch on their oiled fur. Was it fur? Alfonzo wasn't sure. He felt both puffy and bony in comparison to their aerodynamic contours. He rarely, if ever, saw seals.

The bar's decoration was a mix of seafaring golden age, rock-and-roll detritus, and locals-only kitsch. Dark gnarled wood walls curved around like a cave, a burrow, or some seaside-dwelling creature's den. Dust coated rope knots, anchors decorated the walls, and the smell of smoke hung ownerless in the air. Tiny stained-glass windows more symbolic than functional sparkled in the walls. Glass fixtures cast weak yellow circles of light on the tables.

By the time he got to Vivi's table, the elephant had joined the seals and sea lions. He didn't mention her.

Vivi's eyelashes were even longer than he remembered.

"It's you," he said.

They nuzzled politely. He was careful not to linger.

He'd wanted to tell her so many things, but what

came out of his mouth was "So an animal walked into a bar—"

"Alfonzo!"

"And he stayed there my entire childhood."

Vivi sighed, but he could tell she still thought he was funny.

Alfonzo told her the story of everything up to the present: his sad father, school and the dissertation, the basement, Vinograd, the cats and their wall holes, the mayor and his pipes, Mitchell and his plot.

She nodded. It made more sense to her than to him. The more angst-ridden Alfonzo became, the more she relaxed. He felt shame and relief. Which was the right way to go? he asked. How could he manage? What should he do?

"It's going to be okay," Vivi hummed.

"How do you know?" Alfonzo asked. "I mean, do you?"

"How could I?"

"Tell me what's happened to you," Alfonzo pleaded.

Viviana took a deep breath and lifted her ears. "Well, if I go all the way back, after we broke up, I moved in with my parents and cried a lot. I didn't end up going to massage school. Remember that plan? My dad was furious that I wasted the tuition deposit. My mother wanted to get me out of my despair—or out of the house—so she pressured me to take a catering job with their friend's friend, who hired me out of pity. I circled ornate rooms like a small shark. I picked up napkins discarded by purebred socialites.

"The work moved me through planes of reality, from kitchen to ballroom to dumpster and back. Catering renders you half-visible, and acceptable in rooms you would not normally be in. I see why the job is a good cover for spies. I witnessed the rulers of New York misbehaving at weddings, fundraisers, and holiday parties because they considered themselves safe, cocooned with their own kind. I witnessed Trouble Helmsley slapping Conchita Posner beside a glittering rooftop pool. I walked in on the Wolf of Wall Street biting the neck of a hired sheep. My coworkers told me to ignore what I saw; they said it was all consensual, probably. Stay silent, they said. I learned that generally the rich are weak, twisted creatures. I learned to hate them while serving them smoked-salmon canapés. In that time, I lost myself; I did whatever drugs were available and stopped dancing.

"One night I was at a VOLE Foundation fundraiser and a cat guest struck up conversation. He asked me questions. At first, I thought nothing of it—I figured he was hitting on me. But then he began talking about art and the sea. I found out he was Hamish McHamish, one of Cappuccino Guggenheim's lovers. Later in the evening, I was making another round of the room when he called me over to meet Cappuccino. They told my boss they were commandeering me for the night, and she just nodded. They took me outside to smoke catnip."

"Oh, I'm sure they had to twist your leg."

Vivi smiled and fluttered her eyelashes. "I was out

in a parking lot with these two strange animals, and I think this is all a funny story I'll tell friends. I tell them I should go back inside and clean up, and then Cappuccino asked, or demanded really, 'Come and work for me?'"

"What about your class consciousness?" Alfonzo asked.

"I was trading the moneyed hordes for interaction with one rich dog. I was desperate for something new."

"What happened?"

"Cappuccino has a home in Venice. She wanted me to join her staff to sail her boat there."

"But what do you know about sailing?"

"Now, something. Then, nada."

Vivi finished her drink. The bar had emptied, save for the sea creatures. Krithi the elephant activist and Edith had long since gone. A seal at the back table kept glancing their way. Vivi nodded.

"You know everyone around here?" Alfonzo asked.

"You want to leave? I bet you're exhausted."

"But what happened on the boat?"

Vivi ignored the question, and a chest-jumping hiccup robbed Alfonzo of the ability to push dignity. Vivi pulled on her poncho and headed for the door.

26.

Alfonzo realized how drunk he was only when he staggered onto his legs. Vivi seemed sober, though he thought they'd consumed the same amount. He swayed out of the Red Clover behind her. He tried to focus. It was pouring rain. He sensed Vivi waiting for an answer to a question he hadn't heard her ask.

"Hum?"

"I said, is that all you brought?"

It was. In his rush from Gowanus, he hadn't thought about the weather, which he now realized had been a mistake. One should always pay attention to the weather and the seasons, the nuances of water and wind. He was an animal in the world, but he was caught, as usual, thinking too much about all the wrong things.

Vivi's mouth was moving and she was nodding her head. He pantomimed deafness. He took deep breaths as the wet wind smacked him. *Wake up, alpaca.*

Vivi pulled a plastic poncho from her bag and put it over his head. He struggled inside the folds. He felt as though he were beneath a tent. The plastic amplified the rain into a cacophonous, crinkling roar.

Vivi was moving now. There were few lights. Alfonzo had to concentrate not to lose her up ahead.

She stopped so that he could catch up.

"Can we take a cab?"

Vivi just laughed. The streets were deserted. Post-apocalypse empty.

"Fonzo, dear, stay calm."

"But what if I get lost?"

"Stop worrying—rain won't kill you."

"I'm melting!"

"Just shut up, sweetheart."

He giggled.

"We're not far, and when we get home I have your bed all set up."

The rain, already torrential, intensified. Little rivulets ran through his wool. Vivi kept her shoulder pressed to his. He felt they were going toward the sea, through the sea. Alfonzo retreated into memory. He began to babble.

"This makes me think of this myth I read about sky animals. They were constellations who chased one another through the waters of heaven. I remember loving that phrase *waters of heaven*. You know that one?"

He didn't expect Vivi to respond. She was just a shape pushing him along. Fatigue, travel, and fermentation beat at his organs. Talking steadied him.

"In the sky there's the llama and baby llama, toad, fox, partridge, and rainbow snake. Oh, rainbow snake! They keep the world in order, at least according to my mom. I miss her, Vivi. It's unbearable. I miss you. I'm so sorry. I was wretched to you."

Vivi didn't hear him. Alfonzo sniffled in the rain.

"You know, the animals aren't constellations, they're anti-constellations. Rainbow snake! Dark spots instead of stars. They think the South Americans knew both stars and the spaces between stars." He hiccupped. "We knew about dark matter so long ago. I say, *of course* ancient animals understood things! Why do we always assume that there's been progress? It's the modern animals who are regressing, forgetting. Progress is such an absurd fantasy. But I digress."

They'd swerved from a main road onto a path that wound between indistinct dunes, black forms rising up against a black sky. His toes sank in the sand.

"Sky llama is very important because of the trip she makes each night. She descends from the mountains to the ocean, takes a big drink, and carries the water back to share gently in the form of rain. It's a story of evaporation, condensation, and precipitation. I mean, it's true, or anyway, it's an accurate metaphor." He blinked rain from his eyes. "Of course, when the colonizers came, they disrupted the transmission of those stories, called them blasphemous. We can't even know how much the Europeans burned. I think of all the string records lost, the plant notes and woven wisdom. I wonder what these continents would be like now, if they hadn't come. All that living knowledge lost. We've dug ourselves into ignorance."

Vivi glanced at him. She'd pulled the drawstring on her raincoat so that Alfonzo could only make out the tip of her pointed nose. They came to a new fork in the path, but rather than taking either branch, she went straight on.

"I guess what I'm trying to say is"—Alfonzo giggled again to himself as the rain ran down his muzzle—"we're all in the hole, but at least some of us are looking at the stars."

Through the gloom Alfonzo made out they were coming to a wooden door in a wall of boulders. Vivi took out a key and opened it, and they entered with a rush of wind.

Alfonzo found they were sputtering beside a long indoor swimming pool in a room made of blue-grey stone. There were piles of towels and neon breathing masks and flippers. Vivi motioned for him to follow. She showed him to a dark bedroom.

27.

Alfonzo woke to the sun, consciousness's accomplice, prodding his eyelids. He ached between his ears and felt the sour acidic pressure of undigested beer gas in his stomachs. He couldn't remember falling asleep.

He lay in a small room on a bed of fresh straw surrounded by shelves full of art and books and glass sculptures in greens and purples. Beside him was a towel and water to drink. He took these as evidence of Viviana's care. Reflecting on the night before, he was satisfied to find only flecks of embarrassment. Many of his most foolish words had been swallowed by the rain. Shaking himself from the straw, he went to wander for coffee.

He called polite hellos, but received nothing in reply.

The pool room they'd passed by the night before marked one end of the house. The long rectangle of water was a motionless silver turquoise. Sunlight streamed through high windows. The snorkel masks, flippers, and towels were in a configuration different from how he remembered them, and they were wet. They'd been used since the night before.

The dark wood hall was lined with closed doors. Alfonzo strained to catch chatter or any sounds of life.

The household hung suspended in a silence that only he disrupted with hungover grumbles.

He poked his neck around a corner and found a giant, bright enclosure. Actually, the word *giant* was inadequate. Alfonzo had been inside many large spaces. He'd wandered the Met Museum and the central public library. He knew the feeling of vastness. But this was the largest room within a private home he'd ever seen. He wondered if such a place could in fact be a home. Beams and columns divided the space into smaller, but still huge, microclimates. Luxuriant vines hung down from the ceiling. Wood and stone carvings stood sentinel. There were also tree trunks and metal posts repurposed as art. The very distant supporting walls were made of stacks of carved boulders. The roof, far overhead, was made of woven logs and sticks, referencing beaver dams or badger-den design. Colours, carpets, furniture, and hanging lamps communicated obscure moods and purposes for each zone. Potted palms ringed a blue circle painted on the floor. Heaps of moss cushions surrounded a fireplace large enough for an ox to stand inside. A red Mamluk mongoose carpet delineated the record player's territory. Far in the distance a glass wall fitted with small doors separated inside from out. Beyond it were dunes, and beyond the dunes the sea. Now Alfonzo understood the kind of umbrella Viviana was sheltering beneath. Cappuccino Guggenheim was this kind of rich. This kind of rich had always been an abstraction to him. But here it was, and here he was inside it, a teetering interloper.

How like Vivi to end up here, he snuffled to himself.

He used to tease that she was not actually vicuña but rather secretly a mountain goat, perpetually ascending rock walls that looked sheer. Always sure-footed. From the vantage of a regular land-bound creature, her movements defied logic. She got scholarships and talked her way into secret meetings. She had a knack for finding ledges and elegant toeholds. She climbed and climbed. Alfonzo kept wandering.

He wanted to sniff out the rich dog's coffee and drink it with greedy abandon. After what felt like a geological era, Alfonzo found a kitchen. He was still alone. He located coffee, ground some beans from Guatemala, and boiled water.

He reflected that what the rich had were lives with all the edges sanded smooth. They might have wretched relationships, illnesses, internal strife—all the stuff one couldn't avoid—but when it came to the material world, they rarely had to cope with snags. They paid, forced, coerced, or bribed others to smooth things for them. It was a life of cotton wool and bulletproof glass. They were always touching flat, unblemished surfaces without ever coming in contact with rough process, with construction; picking, sorting, and all the other bloody, toe-breaking work must take place before raw material becomes finished product.

Coffee, for instance, was a highly refined fuel. It was one of those nothing-everything commodities that came from destruction, growth, and decay. As with all drugs, a great deal of work and violence took place in order to get it into the body. And once all that happened, the material turned into just a subtle feeling of energy. A passing charge in the nervous system. It took so much to make something into nothing. Animals were murdered so that all these drugs, the clandestine and the legal alike, could be grown and sold. Governments rose and fell over hills of beans.

Coffee was grown in lands where basic food markets were unstable. Alfonzo had studied this with Dr. Vinograd. They'd spent a whole semester talking only of the "open veins" of South America. Very little of the money spent on a product went to the country where it was produced. This was true of coffee and bananas and gold and rare-earth minerals. One could understand that mining was extractive. It depleted the land. But with living things, with growing organisms, the knowledge felt counterintuitive. Plants that in their natural form came and went according to season became in their agricultural form another kind of mining. The banana, for example, became a curse because of its popularity. The northern love of bananas and chocolate and coffee alike became the undoing of its producers. Places with the highest rates of deforestation were the same lands that produced the most coffee.

Encountering only polished things made for easy innocence. The rich never learned, or they wilfully forgot, the raw that came before the cooked. Building warehouses, planting and then picking coffee, making paper bags, packing and unpacking boxes, grocery shopping, washing cups. He thought of the tasks upon tasks that came before and after coffee. Cities would collapse without all this service, maintenance, care. How many advertisers and shops and prisons existed to hide labour and process?

How did you sort it out? Did one brood upon this over breakfast or ignore it? Sometimes in turning away, you end up making a full circle.

Alfonzo laughed at himself. This was why he got in fights at birthday parties. How much was the right amount to know? How should an animal be? What did it take to really be a good boy?

According to the label, this coffee was shade-grown. Alfonzo hummed, *Shade-grown, shade-grown. Never send to know for whom the shade grows; it grows for coffee.* No animal is an island.

Alfonzo thought of his mouldy studio. He remembered the apartment he and Vivi had shared post-college, with its stack of unopened bills and pyramid of half-rinsed recycling. Money smoothed edges. That's why it was easy for the rich to convince themselves that the world was naturally smooth, and that it was the poor who made it jagged. How much did he himself want to forget and unsee?

Alfonzo balanced his hot coffee and almond milk in a cup. The cup rattled, spilled a little.

There was still no one around, so he thought he should amuse himself. Alfonzo put his coffee down by the record player and began to browse the music. The record collection went on and on. There were rare things he'd only ever read about, and countless albums he'd never heard of.

There was *Brokenhearted Dragonflies: Insect Electronica from Southeast Asia, Otter Sounds, Dark Round the Hedges.* There were the recordings of Full Mantis, Max Roach, and Annette Peacock. He flipped past Moon Dog and Chick Corea.

After more searching, Alfonzo decided to play *Josephine: Live.* He was feeling nostalgic, and this familiar voice was what he wanted. Though he'd heard the album many times, the strangeness of Josephine's voice never lessened. Josephine sang like all her kind, yet you could not mistake her voice for another's. Her songs were plain ones about struggle. A long time ago, the rodents had risen up against poisoning and traps, and all the other violence heaped on their heads, and Josephine had been there to sing of it. But through her voice, you came to know how their community constituted itself in crisis and tension. Her society was always about to fly apart, and she sang to hold it together. But the tension of these impulses was almost unbearable, and the toll, too, could be heard in the artist's voice.

Had this been her last concert? Alfonzo imagined it that way because it made the recording more potent. She was an animal before or beyond her time. Other animals recognized what she'd meant only after she was gone and, in truth, not even then. She was a light seen through a hole in a black sheet. She was a compact mirror held up to the starry night. With her singing, she focused the audience. Or was it that their attention focused her? *Are we one or many?* she asked without asking, for her songs were always folksy and full of metaphors. But even as she asked this question, her existence was foregrounded. One mouse stood onstage and demanded singular attention. If they were many, they would all be singing. "Perhaps they admire in her what they do not admire in themselves," a critic said, and perhaps if she could teach them to hear themselves better, Josephine would no longer be needed. The mouse folk required Josephine—whether or not they admitted it—to cherish and hate. That is the role of all singers in an endangered community.

But then again, could Alfonzo really know, separated as he was from that era? They say that to take in her art, one had to not only hear but also see Josephine in the flesh, or rather the fur. The recording was an imperfect substitute. On the back of the album was a black-and-white photo from the concert at which it was recorded. The mouse was small yet powerful on the high-contrast stage. In the background were little faces of the crowd caught in countless frozen expressions that ranged from ecstasy to distraction to incomprehension. Josephine had been called the voice of the voiceless, but from the picture you could see that the voiceless were not that. Were they even one group, or were they a multiplicity of voices who also listened? But yes, Alfonzo thought, they were for an instant a together something, because they allowed themselves to be an audience for her. To listen together. To differentiate the normal songs of work and life from a performance. To gather together around Josephine's sound made them a group, and in that collection maybe they could imagine their collective need, or pain.

He thought of that era, the heady years after Napoleon Herbert's fall, before the birth of his own generation, when his parents and their friends had been young. Josephine's voice reminded Alfonzo of his mother. It made him think of an ambient, collective nostalgia for groups of shaggy animals, large and small, shoulder to shoulder, swaying in the twilight summer of Central Park and humming songs together. They united then in what they were against, but they did not know that their enemies would go after their ability to think of what they were for. It was believed that that era contained a momentary electricity that had dissipated as quickly as it had been generated. They thought they were making a new reality. And they did. It's just that what they ended up making was nothing like what they'd dreamed.

The last song on the album always got him. It was Josephine's most iconic. The hope and power and longing she transmitted with just her piping was almost impossibly poignant. Her delivery was a howl, a hollow envelopment. Her voice made a womb big enough to hold everyone who listened. The mouse was a keening mother. A war mother. An exile mother. A mother made of monochromatic stripes brown, red, and purple. A wailing mother.

Alfonzo's eyes grew hot. He tried to breathe them cool. *Just breathe it out.*

Far off, at the other side of the cavern room, the front door clicked, and Vivi and her friends entered in animated conversation, carrying sacks of food. Vivi's buoyant gaggle invaded the fancy home like they owned the place. For all intents and purposes they were its current possessors. Alfonzo's melancholy skittered away like dust-bunny fluff.

Vivi gave Alfonzo a flurry of details about the others as they unpacked groceries. He caught what he could. There was a badger who took care of the grounds but also had a law degree. There was Tania George, a fluffy brown lynx from Montreal whom Vivi described as an amateur witch and a professional cuddler. Alfonzo asked if professional cuddling was like a sex thing, and Vivi just rolled her eyes.

"He's a dumb joker," Vivi explained.

Roberto Snowy was a scruffy dog artist who had spent years travelling the world.

The final creature Vivi introduced was Flann, whose last name Alfonzo didn't catch, a sleek pig sailor who was the captain of Cappuccino's boat. The boat itself was named the *Man Ray*.

"And what about you?" Flann inquired.

"Vivi didn't tell you? She and I used t-to . . . ," Alfonzo stuttered.

"He and Mitchell are best friends in the city," Vivi volunteered. "He's involved in the leak."

This was how it had always been with Vivi. She befriended the kinds of animals who turned Alfonzo shy and defensive. She was never just herself, but always a part of a larger entity. She gravitated toward the exotic, the beautiful, the radical.

Though Alfonzo had just had his coffee, his companions were thinking about dinner. He realized he'd slept much of the day.

They began preparations for a feast.

"In your honour," Vivi teased.

Alfonzo was ordered to assist Tania. Tania told him they would be in charge of salad, and somehow this carnivore made the task sound endlessly complicated. She demonstrated carrot grating. He did his best not to roll his eyes. He got nervous around predators, even ones on the small side. He didn't want to think about what Tania ate when not in mixed company. His brain got a bit cloudy at the possibilities.

After a little while grating and dicing, Alfonzo worked up the nerve for banter.

"So, Tania, what do you call an alpaca with a carrot in his ear?"

She squinted.

"Anything you want. He won't be able to hear you."

Not even a hint of a smile. Alfonzo began shredding some centipede grass. They set the table with apples, kale, hay, and grainy mash.

Though the group had mostly ignored Alfonzo thus far, once they'd eaten and were dawdling over wine, Vivi's friends started sniffing at him with friendly aggression.

"So, are you here to join us, or is this radical sightseeing?"

"Don't put him on the spot like that."

"Do you feel implicated in what the mayor is doing?"

"Tania, you know better than to believe this is a representative system. And I told you, he and Mitchell are working from the inside."

"But I mean, at what point does it get to be too much? Have you ever considered quitting City Hall over the mayor's rhetoric?"

Alfonzo felt himself getting so wound up, he wanted to spit.

"Where is the outside? I mean, you think I'm inside and you're out?" He knew he should know better.

"Cool down, brother," Roberto said. "You're among friends here."

"Let's all be nice," Vivi admonished. "Alfie's in a sensitive state. He came to learn about SERF."

"Right," Roberto chimed in. "If we want to get him on our side, we can't fight with him."

"Front toward enemy!" Vivi declaimed ironically to break the tension.

Tania said they should toast to that.

28.

The next day, Sunday, Vivi suggested a walk, just the two of them. She lent Alfonzo a sweater. He hardly needed it. The day was clear and mild, warm for November. It rarely felt like the month it was anymore.

Vivi led him down toward the beach.

From the outside Alfonzo saw that the exterior of Cappuccino's house was not so much a structure as a dune with windows. Despite its interior volume, the place almost disappeared into the island. You'd never know it was there, save for the windows' reflections flashing from behind a screen of seagrasses. Even when he studied the building straight on, Alfonzo couldn't tell if it was buried on purpose or by nature. Was it a result of slow disaster or design that winked at disaster? Alfonzo saw that Cappuccino's mound lay between more traditionally designed mansions owned by other millionaires, billionaires, or whatever sort of -aire you had to be to own a piece of beach.

The air moved the sand and turned everything into waves, sand particles and light, bird calls and echoing horns. Nothing was solid. Sand caught in their wool. The land was less land and more loose matter in continual flux. The wind was catching bits of him and carrying them away.

In college, Alfonzo and Vivi had taken a class with a famous bird. The bird was a linguist who focused on time and speech. In one lecture he had explained that Aymara—a language spoken in the Andes—appeared to be the only one in the world in which the past was conceptualized as physically in front and the future behind. What most of us are used to imagining is the past at our back and the future ahead of us. It's so ingrained it feels natural, invisible in the way seasons used to be. The future comes at us, the past recedes at our backs.

In the Aymara framework, by contrast, one moved backward into the future. In that period of college, Alfonzo had been experimenting with mind-altering substances—locoweed, chocolate, catnip. Perhaps it was that, or that this information related to the Andes, but the lecture had struck Alfonzo. One backed into one's life while looking "forward" at history. When Alfonzo considered it, the Aymara conception made more sense than the one we're used to. We've already seen our past, so one might imagine that we're facing it. Our future, however, sneaks up behind us. It leaps out and shocks even the most careful creature. The future is unknown until it grabs us by the tail.

Everyone leaves a trail of their disintegration. Move through time and watch the marks you leave: photographs, cologne whiffs hovering over an empty sidewalk, notes tucked in bicycle spokes, wet footprints in foyers. Flakes of breakfast pastry, stray hairs, eye gunk wiped away, dead cells, dandruff—you are always leaving something behind. Some microns of matter are hard, others very soft. Our bodies slough apart as navel lint, follicular meringue, dried spittle crystals. We leave these crumbs just in case we ever get the chance to return. But we never do. There is no retracing. Everyone falls to pieces eventually. Melancholy is just that experience of backward-looking. Even the most focused, striving prognosticator can't see what will happen next. We back into what's coming, no matter how hard we crane our necks. Aging is our only means of time travel. Winds blow us into the future, and all we leave behind is a collection of decaying mementos.

Be here now, looking back, backing forward, Alfonzo hummed to himself.

Intermittent gusts carried away every other word of the conversations Alfonzo and Vivi tried to have. Were they murmuring to one another or to themselves? Each blink dissolved the positions of objects in relation to one another. Birds hung suspended in the static pressure of competing gusts. Clouds blew between them and the sun.

Vivi gestured to a wooden boat pulled up on the beach. They sat down in its shelter, facing the sea. The grey-green-black waves kept coming and going, never tiring. The waves came. The waves went. Alfonzo imagined all the fish out there and wondered at their shapes, what they saw and heard.

The briny aquatic life odours mixed with decay: plant, animal, and mineral mingled.

Vivi turned to Alfonzo and began to hum a new story.

When I went out to sea the first time, I was terrified. The terror was a constant ringing or groaning within. I was losing my mind. I got so sick I couldn't leave the cabin. It wasn't even that the water was choppy or that there was some real danger. I just had this feeling the trip was the end. I panted and rocked and cried and hummed over what was lost—you, Silvio, my childhood, the idea of my life. Time stretched painfully. I felt I couldn't handle living, and yet I continued breathing. Sleep didn't relieve the pain. Dreams didn't. I couldn't eat or drink. And all the while we were moving farther out to sea.

We sailed, and the inner angst got a little quieter, or rather it got more manageable. Calmed, I began to listen in a new way. I rejoined the crew. They had been busy all during my crisis, keeping us afloat and moving. The other crew had been carrying me, and themselves, on.

Above board I began to notice things about the landscape of the sea. Huge ships passed us by, rocking us like we were a toy. We moved through oil slicks that fouled the hull. Dead birds and fish swirled in the waves. We heard strange booms and felt shocks.

We arrived at a zone of blue water cross-hatched with orange-brown seaweed. I didn't think there could be seas within the sea, but that's what it was. The Sargasso. We'd been sailing south, not west. We stopped and stayed there, still, floating on this edge. I asked what we were doing, but my friends wouldn't tell me. Maybe they didn't really know.

What I began to notice in our stillness was the trash, large and small and smaller still, all mixed into the water. I had heard there were trash islands. That's how they're described in the news, right? I'd always pictured them as solid heaps made of car parts, Styrofoam, and basketballs covered in mussels all wrapped together by rotting ropes. Like a trash mountain that drifted and spun with the tides. I imagined something you could climb. But what I saw was more like a cloud, billows of milky dust in the water. The others told me all the tiny particles were plastics and what kept them together was the Atlantic vortex. I kept watching the sea. The weather was warm. The days and nights were of equal length.

I listened to the VHF radio, and Tania explained what I was hearing. Codes, strings of three letters, squeaks and static and silences. Send three letters and wait for a response. That was how it worked, she told me. It has a poetry to it, a call-and-response musicality.

We sent out a question, to whom, I did not know. We asked, "QOA?" Can you communicate by radiotelegraphy? And after a pause we would hear back, "I can communicate by radiotelegraphy."

We asked, "QOF?" *What is the quality of my signals?* They would reply, "The quality is good."

"QUK?" *Can you tell us the condition of the sea observed?* "The sea is calm with blue mixed sargassum waves," they replied.

We knew they were close. But still we had to wait. We just sat, rocking. Two more days passed like this in undulating stasis. On the third evening, we were sharing stories to pass the time. And just as the orange sun slipped below the horizon, we heard the radio whistle.

"QRV?" *Are you ready?* they called to us. We responded, "We are ready."

Then we asked, "QUP?" *Should we indicate our position by searchlight, black smoke trail, or pyrotechnic light?* We heard back, "No searchlight, black smoke trail, or pyrotechnic light. Just wait."

We asked, "QBH?" *Are you flying below cloud?* But we heard nothing.

Then someone hooted up on deck. We went to see, and there was Bobby Seal. He was profoundly calm. He was glossy black-brown and big, powerful and graceful in his movements. We offered him water, food, whatever we had, but he didn't want anything. He just stared, and we stared back.

After some secret cue, he began to sing. His mouth was

closed, but there were words. It was like humming or
piping, or maybe there wasn't even sound. But we could all
feel the vibrations. The strange thing was, we could
understand him perfectly. We compared what we had
retained and our memories matched. Parts of this foreign
song lodged in our brains. After he'd gone, we tried to write
down what we knew. We tried to keep it all fresh.

Alfonzo found he could hardly breathe. He managed only a whisper. "What did he sing? What was the message?"

The ocean came and went, almost touchable yet infinitely far away. The waves didn't so much crash as relax into the beach. All along the waterline were bits of plastic, slime-coated bags indistinguishable from the jellyfish corpses that lay beside them. Vivi vibrated her subtle body.

29.

Alfonzo and Vivi found her friends whispering back in the kitchen. Roberto and Tania stopped and stared when they entered.

"So?"

"So, what?"

"What have you two been up to? Necking?"

"No! Someone's got to bring him into our cult, right, Robbie?" Vivi said.

"Oh, good, so you're becoming one of us?"

"One of us!" Tania yipped.

Vivi nuzzled her friends, and whispered something to Tania.

"We're going to make dinner, if you want to help out."

They'd been slow cooking Appaloosa beans. Roberto was going to prepare a tagine the way he'd learned in Rabat.

Outside, darkness arrived with wailing wind. The season returned to its traditional form, and Alfonzo snuggled himself into Vivi's sweater. They set candles around the dining room zone of the grand room. Cheap beer and wine and little bowls of herbs and nuts appeared. The animals gathered around the table. They made toasts to togetherness and the unknown. Conversation unspooled. Alfonzo felt embraced by the group.

"What is the task other than to mourn what we know but cannot bear to speak?"

"Well, true acceptance would require so great a change."

"Of what we have become."

"Hum."

"It isn't unsolvable if the Western bubbles change."

"What will it take to change?"

"I don't know, something deafening? Something almost silent?"

"Almost nothing at all."

"I remember when one of Cappuccino's friends commissioned an alchemist bird to make a rhodiola tincture. The alchemist promised it would show the future. Cappuccino took it with her stockbroker. He became obsessed. He kept going back to the bird to get more and more . . ."

"What happened to him?"

"He went insane."

"Wasn't he already?"

"Touché."

"We're all in the same boat, whether we admit it or not."

"A sinking one."

"But also, we're trying to know what we already know. If you think you're exempt, you're wrong. If you think the cities won't sink. If you believe the system isn't a death cult . . ."

"Have you heard about the mass beachings?"

"In the news they're always reported as these mysterious anomalies," Alfonzo offered. "Like, 'The poor creatures are confused,' or 'Look at these evil beasts out to get us.'"

"The sea animal is not some mystical other."

"Ice is melting into the sea."

"These are the facts!"

He felt Vivi staring, and he tried to hum some vague ideas. It was hard to keep up with radical thinking. He'd been trapped in the city while Vivi was travelling. She could sail off to Venice and come up with sweeping theories about economics and ethics, but he was stuck in the city, in his studio apartment, his basement job. This was not his beach, he hummed.

"Some of us don't have the luxury of living our ideals," he said, hating himself even as he expressed that idea. This was not how he wanted to be.

They weren't reaching for luxury, only survival, someone responded.

The late grew later. They cleared and washed dishes. They laughed more. Fighting was okay. Bad jokes were okay. They argued about records, and someone turned up the volume. Alfonzo realized that whatever answers he wanted he would not get, and so it was better to just relax. Roberto poured strong mysterious drinks, and Tania rolled catnip joints that they smoked outside in the cold wind. The seagrasses bent and relaxed. They played and danced in the huge living room, sliding across the wood floor and falling into pillows. Someone put on the Flowers

Group and then followed that with the hits of Princess Nicotine. They danced to Malagasy soul and scorpion pop. Alfonzo asked again about the sea music, but the others only head-butted in response.

"Just enjoy your time," Tania told him. They all passed out on the floor in a heap.

Alfonzo had a vivid dream. There had been an earthquake. Old, once-marvelous edifices lay crumbled. A herd of animals was constructing a fountain out of the wreckage.

The animals rushed to and fro in great excitement, gathering bits of green copper pipe and statuary. Here a spouting dolphin, there the leg of a bronze horse. The creatures explained to Alfonzo that the Panda-brand bottle conglomerate had donated the water for the fountain. Alfonzo was tasked with pouring the bottles' contents into the fountain. The animals got more and more fevered as the dream went on. He struggled to keep up.

"We must finish," one declared.

"No," another said, "we're just starting."

Then he heard this sea song. It was a dream, but at the same time, it wasn't.

30.

See.

The sea.

The sea exists as unknowably radical life expanse.

The sea exists as stretching groundswells, as brine life, capricious and dainty.

See the sea's surfaces as a storm-flapping tent that glows from within green gold and blue-black.

See, light exists. Exists in the form of sun waves falling as reflection and scattering.

Light falls into sea, and sea's murk transubstantiates. Light food disappears into our heaving green-black folds. All who are in, who are all, eat the sea's murk or eat one another with reverence. So, we in the sea see that we all eat the light's waves, in a way.

In the sea sounds exist. Sounds more than exist. The sea resonates with itself and with us. The sea is a shell that resounds with us.

Walls of coral, ceilings of ice, ocean floors reflect and return our sounds enriched. The sea possesses deep channels like radios. Sound travels faster in the sea. Sounds circle through our radio waves.

Sea is our vessel and the vessel is a medium and the medium is a clear gel for growing culture. Sea exists, so vessels exist, so culture exists, so media exist, which makes us media makers.

We are media makers who sing, who steer ourselves with song in the craft of breath control. We are microtone traders who compress under pressure. Great pressures exist. We sing the world exists circularly in songs. We all hear.

Somewhere we sing and hear others who hear and sing somewhere. We are sea herds hearing singing in ways and we sing now to you who live just over the wet lip of the dry land.

What is sung in the Atlantic gyre is heard in the Barents Sea; and what is sung in the Barents Sea is heard in the North Pacific; and what is sung in the North Pacific is heard in the Bay of Bengal; and what is sung in the Bay of Bengal is heard in the Atlantic gyre. It goes circularly like this.

This song is for your benefit. This is a benefit concert sung in your language, so that you don't mistake it. We have to start somewhere with you. We are starting somewhere.

We would wish nothing more than to sing and to go on singing always about the sea and how the light falls through the murk and the way our sounds circle, but we must turn toward something else. We must sing of death.

These songs we have sought to flee are following us circularly. We ask you to listen. Listening does not exist, it is only practised. We ask you to practise, please.

We sing of strands of poison in food that is life.

Marine grasses exist. Marine grasses exist as one form of our sunlight-fed murk that we eat. Marine grasses exist undulating in beds where we eat and sleep and hide and dream. Marine grasses have roots, and leaves and marine grasses produce flowers and seeds, like the flowering plants of your gardens. Our plants are anchored by root systems, and the root systems of marine grasses buffer the dry lands against hurricanes.

Plastic exists. Plastic exists as we know, and keeps existing and circling endlessly as a song but poison. It echoes the shapes and motions of food, so we eat it. Bottle caps, drinking straws, little red-orange bits that look like food but nourish no one. It catches us and clings. It disintegrates and mixes, and we eat it. We can't see it, and we eat it. Plastic seems to exist forever, and its particulated weight is breaking us. Break us open and see we're full.

It is so difficult to sing to make others see, but we try as our numbered losses exist and grow.

Stress exists and poisons exist.

Oil is the precious poison made of hydrocarbons and heavy metals, and hydrocarbons and heavy metals cause cancers and deaths. Oil disrupts the hearing and singing of small vital plants and small vital animals. It gathers in organs and lingers on leaves for longer than we can measure. Oil is refined and spilled everywhere. Oil coats our seagrasses, which exist as our deep green beds. When seagrass dies it washes ashore the animals who take refuge in the grasses and die from ingesting the residue that clings. Oil is spilling everywhere constantly, not just in disaster forms but drop by drop by drop without notice.

Accumulation exists.

Heat exists and grows. Stress exists and poisons exist. Where there is too much noise and heat and stress and poison to bear, our bodies wash ashore and you see them. We see you see us. We play this record back.

Scratch into the record a seal, then add one more. Record then the dying sounds of two dolphins, three right whales, five humpbacks, eight pilot whales, and thirteen more dolphins. But we have barely begun with the spiralling line because death has added to its sound twenty whales and one dolphin, which equals twenty-one, and then thirty turtles and four whales, which equals thirty-four.

And it does not stop there, but turns and adds to the ever-turning forty-one more humpbacks and nine turtles and five sperm whales, which equals fifty-five. And even then, the sounds grow by eighty-six turtles and three dolphins, which equals eighty-nine. Another turn adds one hundred and six turtles and thirty-eight dolphins, which equals one hundred forty-four.

There are one hundred sixty-seven dolphins, and thirty turtles, and twenty-three whales, and nine turtles, and four whales, which equals two hundred thirty-three.

Then there are the three hundred fifty minke whales and twenty-seven pilot whales, which equals three hundred seventy-seven.

And we cannot stop even there, for there are more to add to the song with the sounds of three hundred turtles, and two hundred forty-three seals, and fifty-six whales and dolphins, and nine more turtles, which equals six hundred eight all dead.

These are only the scratches we know. And you see how death's groove spirals toward the uncountable. There are tons of bodies, masses of corpses, heaps of creatures we have known who now exist only dead.

Is your mind slipped over with a numbness that grows until

you cannot feel your limbs? It is too much to count. We sing, we know.

We have tried and tried adapting, swimming ceaselessly through these ever more leaded waters. We have seen you too trying and tiring. But we cannot do much more. So from the soaking edges we sing. We sing to you who are also struggling.

We have fins that are old legs. You have legs that are former fins. And we see that you with your legs have charity runs to look for cures to cancers and sadness and madness. And when you run for charities, you drink water out of little disposable bottles of plastic, and the water in those bottles is full of plastics and metals that give you cancer. This is not kind, just true.

We in the sea have a habit of smelling and tasting one another's shit to check if we are healthy and we can sing we're not healthy.

We have cancers, cancers and sadness and madness that cling. We have memories stored in our fats alongside poisons. We have stresses and cancers from the plastics and oils inside. We have fish feelings, or let's just call them feelings.

Fish have feelings.

We sing to you to say, "Hey, stranger to yourself, remember, this language is no shell game."

Beneath these word-shells are soft bodies.

You are singing animals and this is communal music that makes it possible to see and share; we see the sick seas rising and dying and we are together terrified. We see sides parched and oversaturated. Warming and endless circling of poisons is happening.

Lead and mercury from oil are in our water, which is your water, or what it is, just water that exists. Water exists within and without you.

We sing all we know.

We sing the wet crisis.

From the soaking edge of the world we sing, we see the sea, and see you are animals who see the sea. We sing to say please. We turn on the record and weep our plastic-flecked salt tears.

We sing because the system will not just naturally change, so we must sing to change it. Sing to see the sea in yourself. Form bands to survive. If you see something, sing something, and if you sing something, sing like you mean it. We must change our lives to live. We sing all this to help you see, imperfectly, but as best we can.

Because if ever there were a time for this, this is it.

Sing with us with your whole seeing being, "This is it."

31.

"It's Monday morning. You have to go home, baby."

Vivi sat beside Alfonzo, nudging him awake. He kept his eyes closed, as if his dreams might leak out if he opened them. He wanted to keep the sad sensation. With their time now too short, Vivi hummed about their past. She hummed that he would always be a part of her herd. Big tears welled. He was one of everyone. By marking him as a part of her herd, she transformed him. He was not the old unbearable love; he was a member of the group. As if everyone were equal in this survival struggle. Just an animal among animals leading their beautiful lives.

"You can't miss the boat."

The glass wall glowed with the grey light of coming dawn. Vivi made tea, and the light outlined the steam spiralling from the travel mug. She pushed him out the door and along the path to the ferry terminal. *Stay*, he thought desperately.

Clouds were gathering above. Clouds were llamas swelled with water, ready to cry on the seas and cities. The clouds moved into the unknown, and he followed. He was ready to jump into the ocean to see if he could swim. Everyone was connected. Vivi didn't speak. He watched her walk before him. All his concentration squeezed into a droplet.

"I can't believe it ends like this," he said.

"It doesn't."

At the dock Alfonzo and Vivi entwined their necks. The ferry dog called out for him to come if he was coming, then pulled a rope across the entryway, separating shore and boat.

And that was it.

The ferry took him to the train that would take him to the city.

Alfonzo slouched into a seat facing away from the direction of travel. See the disasters piling up behind as you are blown backward into the uncertain future. Breathing deeply, he removed his notebook from his satchel. In a trance, he transcribed. He was not the writer or the singer. He was simply the scribe.

When he finished, he tore out the leaves, crumpled them, put them in his mouth, and chewed. He would digest what he had heard. He would teach himself a lesson. Absorb it. Use it for fuel. He was just one channel. He was just an alpaca moving messages from beyond, back into himself, through himself, all so he could pass along what the sea sang into him.

SARDINES

32.

The train retraced its path from the End of the World back to the centre of everything. The repeating backyards grew smaller and smaller the closer the train drew to the city. Somewhere in Brooklyn the yards vanished and were replaced by apartment walls. The clouds greyed overhead. The train went underground, and Alfonzo, a thoroughly chewed-up morsel, was finally deposited deep in Atlantic Station.

Deliriously tired, he threaded through the tunnels. There was no time to go home for fresh clothes and coffee. City Hall expected him. He knocked an old goat off balance and stuttered a sorry. He waited for an R train, which was delayed because of an earlier incident. The one that finally heaved up to the platform was stuffed to the gills. He shoved on with more apologies. The conductor barked at everyone to stand clear. Beneath his legs, a flock of pigeons gathered in; he locked his knees and cast his gaze downward.

Alfonzo wondered how he was supposed to get through this new day after everything. But then, what was this *everything*? He'd visited an old love and her friends, they'd talked feelings and politics, and then he'd had a dream. He was just one random alpaca whose life, as far as he knew, was still normal. Normal in its constraints. The change was within.

He surfaced finally at City Hall Station. A light snow had started falling askew from the matte grey clouds. At the top of the stairs, Alfonzo made eye contact with an old llama who wore the same judgmental expression as his father. Luis's voice rang in his mind's ear. *Say whatever you want to friends. Transcend on the weekend with drinks and song. Attend protests and dream lucidly every night. Do whatever you want, but do it on your own time. No matter what, make sure you're where you're paid to be come Monday morning. You've got to be responsible.*

Dark-coated animals circled the empty fountain. Their footprints wrote lines across the snowy paving stones. Among them was an alpaca with her scarf knotted the way Alfonzo's mother used to do hers. These were workers who behaved themselves, and here he was, among them.

But for what? he argued with his inner father. Have I come dutifully to be fired? If I'm lucky, I've come to be shuffled to another basement office, to yet another windowless room where I'll live in fear of leaks and mould and the ceiling's collapse. I come to watch the slow damp rot the records of our existence. Am I an animal who does what I'm told out of fear? *You do your job*, his inner father hummed. *The big picture is above your pay grade. You behave yourself so you'll have a home to dream in.*

All around him, animals disappeared. They were there

moving along, clear to him one instant, then a door opened and they were gone, swallowed by an office tower.

Humming, Alfonzo turned away from City Hall. *Dad*, he reassured his mental father, *you're not my enemy. You don't have to be afraid.* He would be responsible soon, he promised, but in a new way. Work wasn't working like it should, so the worker must change.

Get a coffee, Alfonzo soothed himself. *Survive the day.*

The Early Cenozoic was empty—not unusual for this time of the morning.

The owners must have brought in more plants over the weekend, or else Pamella had a wild way with flora. For whatever reason, the café felt equatorial. Orchid stalks arched their purple and orange flowers toward the windows. Staghorns pointed their apple-green leaves every which way. Peace lilies in terracotta stood guard beside the bathroom, and a fern suspended in macramé tickled at a golden pothos that had climbed up the wall with the aid of its little brown stem toes. The lemur barista was barely visible amid the foliage. Familiar noises pulsed low, beneath traffic noise from the street.

"Is this Akida?" Alfonzo called out as a way of making his presence known.

"Oh." Pamella emerged from the leaves. "I've been waiting for you, Mr. Faca."

"Mr. Faca is my father. You can call me Al."

Pamella jumped from plant to counter and ducked

beneath. There was a rustling sound, and the lemur returned clutching a stack of newspapers.

"These are for you," she said.

Each paper had bold full-page spreads, and each trumpeted the same story. Unlike the usual coverage of Mayor Shergar, in these photos the horse looked sweaty and spooked. There were shots of the mayor rearing back, away from a swarm of microphones, and showing the whites of his eyes. Alfonzo studied the headlines.

SHOCKING REVELATIONS: OUR FULL
COVERAGE OF THE CITY HALL LEAKS
SEADYNE SLIPPED MAYOR MILLIONS
THROUGH OFFSHORE SHELLS
SECRET DOCUMENTS SHOW ADMINISTRATION
CAUGHT IN FINANCIAL TRAP; SHERGAR
DENIES ALL

They had done it. Or really, Mitchell had done it. He looked to Pamella, and her expression told him this was real.

"You should have seen City Hall when I opened this morning," Pamella said. "Black cars coming and going. All kinds of sinister swine scuttling in and out. There were a million reporters, but security cleared them from the steps before they hustled the mayor out in blinders."

"Who was taking the mayor away?" Alfonzo asked.

"Oh, you know. The *really* powerful ones," Pamella replied. She was calm. "Can I fix you something? We'll look more natural if I'm making a coffee. You never know who's watching."

Alfonzo's stomachs contracted. He was hot in his wool.

They were in it together. They were all enmeshed, caught in a system they'd been born into. There was no going backward. The stereo continued to chirp out music. Where was Mitchell?

"This is huge, isn't it?" Alfonzo wanted Pamella's reassurance. "Maybe this will change everything? I mean, isn't this how revolutions start?"

"Perhaps." Pamella nodded with a little snort.

"You're not convinced."

"I'll tell you a story." She twisted a knob, and a cloud of steam escaped from her machine. "Where I grew up, each election brought some fresh scandal and violence. With each turn, a new figure would appear to promise, 'It will be different now.' And then they would collude with the old guard to ensure things stayed the same.

"For many generations, our kind accepted this because it was balanced with the beauty of our home. It was the plants and animals of our community that made life livable; politics was a farce we laughed at. You can't understand the riches we had around us. There were fruit orchards. There were peanuts, the best passion fruit, and tamarind and guava. Everyone had a garden. Even the poorest had lushness within claw's reach."

Pamella purred in fruit reverie.

"But little by little coffee began to replace the other crops. At first, we hardly noticed, but then the coffee owners began to want more. They wanted everything. Our whole community moved, but the landowners also wanted the place we moved to. This process continued until we wound up pushed to the coast."

"Is that when you came here?" Alfonzo asked.

"No, no. First the comedy had to get worse. There was a scandal. The president was lining his bank accounts with coffee money. And despite all the land deals, the treasury was a hollow shell. I remember how angry my father was. He was a citizen, he fumed. He was a respectable lemur who obeyed the law, but this was too much. He went out onto the streets to join the animal masses. They stampeded to the presidential palace to protest against coffee. A snap election was called. We rejoiced. The opposition party gained a wave of followers when they promised—they swore on their mothers' bones—that a vote for them was a vote against coffee."

"What happened?"

"The opposition won. We believed that this time we, the regular animals, had won. The coffee growers were compelled to leave. My mother dared to suggest that we might return to our home territory. The new party seemed to be keeping their word until they quietly began to roll out a new plan. The coffee lands would be replanted with tea. The economy would run on tea, which they assured us was much healthier and more patriotic. 'Tea is not coffee,' the new president beamed from the TV sets, and no one could say he was lying."

Alfonzo couldn't breathe right. The coffee-shop air smelled of yeast, pipe tobacco, and malt. It smelled of owners' houses and pickers' shacks. It smelled of chocolate and dung and matted earth and scented candles.

"But then what was the point? Didn't you feel hopeless?" Alfonzo asked.

"What else were we going to do but struggle?" Pamella replied. "It's a choice between hope and hopelessness. We aren't against the mayor because we support his opponents. We don't want tea as a solution to coffee, or pig proposals to solve horse problems. If a seal were to somehow become the mayor according to the rules as they are now, that wouldn't be victory. The struggle has always been life and death, I suppose, but it feels different now, in that we— you and I and everyone we care for—we won't have a home that's not underwater, we won't have unpoisoned food or air if we don't struggle. Some say the rich will feel the rising seas, too, but you can be sure they'll be the last to get wet, by which time it will be too late for the rest of us. We can't keep running in their hamster wheel."

The bell above the door tinkled.

A llama walked into the café, and it was Mitchell. He wore sunglasses despite the lack of sun and a grey scarf wrapped all the way up to meet the bucket hat that covered his ears. This was his disguise for the City Hall goons who didn't seem to be looking for him. He was a beautiful, absurd creature. The three were happy to be reunited. Alfonzo sniffed away his sadness as Pamella embraced Mitchell's long neck. Their friendship was so fragile and necessary.

Mitchell said they should take a walk to be out in the weather.

Pamella wrote a note, BACK SOON!, and taped it to the door. They left the music playing and the lights on and ambled out onto the street.

The clouds above were black and blue and grey all over, low as they arrived from the north. Most of all, the clouds were wet. The snow they'd been producing had turned to something else, a shifting foggy rain. The snow had become an explosion of particles too insubstantial to bother with gravity.

The city followed the weather's lead. Greasy steam burst from exhaust vents. Workers puffed on break-time cigarettes. Their smoke rushed upward to join its god, the clouds. Tires sliced puddles, and the sprays hit pedestrians who were wielding umbrellas as shields. The mist caught in fur and feathers and soaked them through. Animals leapt to stay dry-footed, but it was futile. Water streamed down the glass-and-steel cliffs and through the concrete valleys. Frigid pools formed around storm drains. Alfonzo dodged custodians sweeping water toward the street with long squeegees. Particles flew into his eyes. He blinked and sputtered.

Mitchell strolled along with Pamella on his back, cool and collected, as if they were stars in some broken version of *Singin' in the Rain*.

Alfonzo recalled the storms of seasons before and the strange, festive mood that would precede them. Everyone turned giddy with the fear of the clouds. He remembered the sandbags heaped around buildings, wood blocking windows, water blurring windshields. He remembered his mother's frail voice over the phone saying they were fine and the restful quality of darkness that fell across the river after that transformer exploded. *We have already heard of what's coming,* he thought. *The music has already begun.*

Into the fancy vestibules of finance buildings the water crept. The water took the cracks and hung on to coats and tails. It slicked across elevator floors and evaporated once inside, steaming up the windows. Droplets sank into carpets in solidarity with the waves that beat against the island's edges. The ice melted, and as it did it sang its song of praise and mourning.

The water would continue to come and go, advancing and retreating at the moon's urging forever. This was not a threat, it was a promise. This was not a battle, just a rhythm.

How long it takes to navigate this tiny fragment of land—eons, perhaps. Mitchell and Pamella whispered and joked between themselves, and Alfonzo trailed behind. They wandered past the bull and all the way to the foot of the Museum of the American Indian. They did nothing to distinguish themselves from the tourists or the other locals. Everyone was wet and therefore vulnerable. *We who are fragile must become willing to change form even as our purpose remains constant,* Alfonzo hummed. They allowed themselves to just belong. They turned east, taking Beaver to Wall, Wall to Water, then finally passed beneath FDR Drive and reached Pier 11.

Under a curve of decorative metal meant to evoke the

prow of a ship was a booth, and in the booth crouched a ticket-seller cat dressed in an orange raincoat. She gave them news of the next ferry, which would sail for Brooklyn. It was 11:00 a.m. now. Their ship would arrive at any moment. Mitchell, Pamella, and Alfonzo thanked her for the good word, and the damp cat scowled from beneath her hood.

This city bobbed and swayed. The wide river, the tidal strait, and the salty waters of the sound hummed in concert. So many millions of creatures lived across this archipelago. They were alive right then in their vulnerable habitat, but it could all just disappear. Alfonzo was not up for the catastrophe. He was just a dumb animal making noises. Thinking of his father, remembering his mother, marvelling over all those he loved, he saw his city. Anything can be a boat as long as it floats.

Praise the craft, Alfonzo hummed. *Praise the shoreline and the harbour. Praise this island with its pizza joints and its music clubs open late. Praise the wounded families who struggle. Praise friends and their couches lent for sleeping when it was not possible to sleep at home. Praise the employed and unemployed, the infirm and the well. Praise the steep hills of the Bronx, the oddly numbered streets of Queens, and the ponds of Brooklyn, blue-green with algae. Praise the animals and the storm which envelopes them. Praise today, what has passed, and all that is to come.*

They huddled together in this blur of water dust. It was not snow or hail or rain or wintry mix, it was just water that had been circling the Earth for a long time, taking many forms. The unnameable mist enfolded the llama, the lemur, and the alpaca. Out in the river they saw the outline of the ferry becoming more solid as the boat approached the land.

They felt happy without knowing why.

ACKNOWLEDGEMENTS

Since the first flickerings of this book, I have been the beneficiary of so much support. Writing arises out of, and feeds into, my relationships with others. Friends and strangers have engaged in conversations and shared nuanced feedback, anecdotes, and their best puns. They not only humoured but also took seriously my insatiable desire for animal talk. I only hope I have done their collective and individual brilliance some justice. It takes a herd.

Thank you, Allison Devereaux, Jeremy M. Davies, Deborah Ghim, Alexis Nowicki, and everyone at FSG for the expert shepherding. Thank you, Hazel Millar and Jay MillAr at Book*hug for their steadfast support of my work. Writing and publishing are complex and I feel fortunate to have met so many kind and committed people through the process.

Thank you, Erin Robinsong, Stephanie Acosta, Erin Dowding, Tricia Middleton, Caroline Picard, Aaron Boothby, Lani Hanna, Sara Clugage, Kristi McGuire, Cat Tyc, Bett Williams, Elizabeth Callaghan, Daniel, Paul, and Joanna Mehrer, Steve Cooper, Banoo Lashai, Josh Peskowitz, Sophie Harris, Corey Frost, Jacob Wren, Chris Kraus, Lisa Locascio, and Ariana Reines.

Thank you, Eugene Lim, for the book's title and for such generous literary guidance and encouragement. Thank you to Maya Smelof, Andy Matinog, and all my fellow students at Red Crow Yoga Shala. Thank you to all the animals I have known, but especially Z-Bat, Greycat and Chicken, Toulouse, Fiona, and Alfons.

Deepest gratitude and love to my family, Geri Murphy, Jessi Hazard, Ruby and Opal Campbell, and my father, Bruce Blevins, who passed on to another plane during the writing of this book, yet remains present and powerful.

And finally, endless love to Rob Callaghan, without whom this book would not exist. It was from him I first learned of Mitchell-Lama housing, which was the door to a labyrinth, and he has been with me in it ever since. He is a consummate and kind New Yorker, an artist in worker's clothing, and a comrade in the most profound sense.

Joni Murphy is from New Mexico and lives in New York. Her debut novel, *Double Teenage*, was published in 2016 and was named one of the *Globe and Mail*'s 100 Best Books of the year.

COLOPHON

Manufactured as the first Canadian edition of
Talking Animals
in the fall of 2020 by Book*hug Press

Copy edited by Stuart Ross
Cover design by Tree Abraham
Text by Jay Millar
Author photo by Erin Dowding